DARK HUNGER

DARK HUNGER

DON JAMES

CUTTING EDGE

ISBN-13: 978-1-962896-99-3

Published by
Cutting Edge Books
PO Box 8212
Calabasas, CA 91372
www.cuttingedgebooks.com

CHAPTER ONE
MILES SALIN

M iles Salin discovered her one Spring morning when the sun was just beginning to be hot enough for sunbathing. From his upstairs window in the rooming house he could look through an opening of newly budded tree branches and have a complete, unobstructed view of the side of the old house on the other side of the street.

He glanced through his window at about eleven o'clock this Sunday morning and saw the woman stretched out on a sun cot. For a long time he looked at her from the concealment of his room, seeing the whiteness of her skin against the dark, one-piece bathing suit that she wore; the contours of her body as she lay quietly, or turned for an even exposure to the sun.

Occasionally she rubbed oil on her skin. She was a trim, slim woman with a pert and exciting fullness of breasts, an impudent roundness of buttocks and a litheness of limbs that filled him with a deep and restless excitement.

Shortly before noon a man, obviously her husband, came out and talked with her while he smoked a cigarette. He was thin with a slight body and none of the physical perfection of his wife. Miles wished he would go back into the house, and was pleased when he did.

A little later the woman went inside and Miles studied the side of the house. Narrow double windows had been remodeled into single large windows. One upstairs probably was a bedroom window, he thought. It had white, sheer curtains, and after the woman had gone into the house he was certain that he saw movement behind the curtains.

He looked down at the street and across the intervening yards and realized that the trees shielded the window from the street. Only from his room was there an unobstructed view of the window, and he knew that his own window would be obscured by the shadow of his rooming house.

The woman did not reappear and finally Miles stopped watching. Later in the day he walked by the house, noting the address. He decided to look in the city directory at the library and find out more about the people who lived in the house.

Miles Salin was tall, well-built, blond and in his late twenties. He had been born and reared on the West Coast, and he lived in a West Side rooming house that was an old mansion converted into a multiple dwelling of weary and worn single rooms. No one in the place bothered him much, and this was the main reason why he stayed there.

Occasionally he worked at odd jobs, when he could find them, or in one of the plywood mills. Sometimes he worked at gas stations, and lately he had worked at a downtown parking lot. This job suited him for the time being and he thought he would probably stay with it, at least until the winter months.

He read a great deal and he watched television on a small 17-inch set in his room. From a magazine about popular electronics he learned how to substitute earphones for the loudspeaker, so he could watch television as late as he wished without receiving complaints from the other roomers.

Hidden on the top shelf of his closet in the room was a small pile of pornographic photographs that he had bought from a man who had brought them from Japan. Sometimes Miles got them out and studied them intently, his mind abandoned to erotic orgies of imagery.

On the streets, at his job, from his room window, and wherever he could, he watched women and fitted them individually into the mental pictures that were so easy for him to conjure up.

He had a high school education, and he had a fairly good intellect. He did well on jobs when he wanted to work. He was probably better read than most of the men with whom he associated on the job. In some fields he was especially well read, and he had bought every book that he could find about sex. Most of these were cheap editions of books ostensibly published for newlyweds. He studied the clinical descriptive passages and he wished that he had a girl who would study them with him.

He had never had a girl. That is, a sweetheart. He had bought girls for a few dollars, and he sometimes tried to experiment with them, but they were indifferent and highly commercial about sex. He wished he could have a girl that he didn't have to buy. But he did not want a wife. This was a responsibility and a condition that frightened him and filled him with a certain revulsion; to the extent that he carefully avoided the casual dates or friendships with girls that might eventually lead him into a betrayal of himself.

He often stood stripped in front of the long mirror in his room and contracted the muscles of his back and shoulders, the sinews of thighs and legs, and studied the lean, powerful lines of his body in the mirror. In addition, he exercised faithfully when he was not on a job requiring physical labor.

His friendships among men were as infrequent as they were among women. He was pleasant and he acted in such a manner that most people liked him. But he stopped it there, and developed a friendship only to the point where it enabled him to hold a job.

His parents had been killed in a highway accident when he was a freshman in high school, and he had lived with an aunt and uncle in a small coast town until his graduation. He had left for the city to enter a branch of the state university, hoping to work his way through school. He had not finished the first year, and had left to take a series of odd jobs.

He did not know what he wanted to do with his life, and thought little about it. All he wanted was enough to eat, a place to sleep, books to read, his television, and someday a woman to do with exactly as he wished.

Specifically he wanted a woman like the young woman who lived in the old house halfway down the block across from the rooming house.

On the Sunday evening that Miles discovered her, he watched television and occasionally looked out his window at the old house. Lights were on downstairs. Shortly after eleven o'clock when he looked, he noticed a light burning in the upstairs room. He felt a stirring of excitement when he saw that the blind was not drawn. Quickly he turned off the television set and the light in his room and returned to the window.

He could see twin beds, a dresser, a doorway, and most of the interior. A bed lamp glowed on a table between the beds and, as he watched, the woman stepped into view. She wore panties and a bra and as he stared through his own window she took off the bra and then stepped out of sight again toward another part of the room.

When she came back she was wearing a very short night-gown. After standing in front of the dresser mirror to look at herself and fluff up her hair, she slipped into one of the beds. A moment later the man came into view wearing pajamas. He got into the other bed and turned out the light.

For ten minutes or so Miles watched the darkened window. Finally he pulled his blind and turned on the TV set again, but he couldn't concentrate on the picture. The excitement was very strong in him, and he stared with glazed eyes at the screen, not realizing that he had failed to put on the earphones he had connected for sound.

The next day during his lunch hour he walked to the library to check the street address of the old house in the city directory. The names were William Camman and Mary Jo Camman. William Camman worked for a news service, and his wife was employed by an insurance firm. Miles noted the address of the insurance firm.

After he left the library he strolled to a large department store and visited the camera department. A sale was in progress and the department was on the main floor where traffic was heavy. On a counter was a display of binoculars, made in Japan and priced fairly low for the special sale.

Several customers were inspecting them, and one man tested a pair by focusing them across the interior of the store. Miles picked up a trim, small pair and focused them on a display near a far wall. The glasses were more powerful than he had anticipated, and he looked at the price: $27.95. He couldn't afford them.

He glanced around furtively. The clerks were busy and a surge of noonday shoppers crowded past. Acting on a sudden impulse, he turned slightly and slipped the binoculars under his coat and was relieved to find that they would fit into an inside pocket. Afterward, he turned and walked out of the store. No one stopped him.

That night he watched for the light to come on in the bedroom across the street. When it did, he darkened his own room and used the glasses. This time the woman disrobed beside the dresser.

Miles watched intently through the glasses and a soft, intense whisper of obscenities issued from his lips while his excitement mounted to a fever pitch.

By July he had learned a great deal about the Cammans. He knew that Bill Camman worked until 2:00 A.M. every third Saturday. He knew the nights they usually made love. He knew the way Mary Jo dressed and undressed; the way she stooped over when she put on a bra; the fact that she seldom wore a girdle and most often a garter belt; that she brushed her hair fifty strokes almost every night; that she sometimes stood naked in the bedroom and carefully inspected her body in the long mirror mounted on a closet door that was barely visible from Miles' room.

He also knew that Bill Camman always dressed hurriedly; that he wore jockey-type briefs and T-shirts under his dress shirts. Sometimes he read in bed—more often than his wife did.

But, most of all, he came to know and savor the intimate, feminine contours of Mary Jo's body. During the days when he was at work at the parking lot he would look at other women and mentally compare them with Mary Jo. Invariably he came to the conclusion that Mary Jo was the woman he would like to have and to own—even if only for a few moments.

Miles' fantasies became more vivid as the days passed and he devised a game of imagining what he would like to do with her. After a time the moves in this exciting pastime began to fit into a pattern that was logical because Miles always managed everything and Mary Jo was completely at his mercy.

The inherent and intriguing possibilities in the game eventually gave rise to speculation about transforming his wild fantasies into reality until, at last, his facile mind created a definite plan of action.

The first phase of the operation was put into effect during a Friday noon rush hour in August when he visited a large department store and bought a pair of dark gray work coveralls. Afterward, he went to a dime store and purchased some wide adhesive tape, a roll of two-inch bandage, a length of clothesline and a pair of women's cotton hose.

He hid his purchases in a pay locker at a bus station near the parking lot. After he finished work he retrieved them and stored them in various pockets in his clothing, with the exception of the wrapped coveralls which he carried in his hand.

Inside his room he unwrapped the packages. He used a pair of scissors to cut one of the stockings. He experimented until he was satisfied with it, then put the cut section of hose in a hip pocket of the coveralls.

From a dresser drawer he brought out a pair of leather dress gloves. He slipped them on his hands, inspecting the palms with a nod of satisfaction.

In the next room Thelma Jorgson turned on her radio and dance music sifted through the wall in muffled cadence. Miles smiled as he wondered what Thelma Jorgson would think if she knew what he intended to do.

She was another one. She with her long legs and blonde hair; with her approaching middle age and her small talk about the doctor's office where she had worked as a receptionist for ten years. She probably knew quite a bit about sex, he thought. She probably read the doctor's books, and the case histories. And she probably wished she had a man. But not Miles Salin. This was too close to home. She could use her friendly glances and her friendly small talk and her small excuses to knock at his door, but he wanted no part of her.

Removing the gloves, Miles put them in the other hip pocket of the coveralls, then folded the garment and placed it in the bottom drawer of his dresser. Next he cut several lengths from the clothesline and placed them on top of the coveralls with the adhesive tape and the bandage. Then he placed several shirts over the collection and closed the drawer.

Now he was ready.

CHAPTER TWO
MARY JO

Mary Jo Camman put the 1955 Ford in the garage beside the old house that they had bought the preceding year. She took out the groceries from the supermarket, carried them through the back door into the kitchen and put them away.

The interior of the old house had been completely renovated by Mary Jo and Bill with a careful regard for colors, drapes, rugs and built-in cabinets. They liked the house and, although the neighborhood was old, it was respectable and close to the center of town.

There was a large, surrounding yard and old maple trees in the front. Bill had built a patio with an outdoor fireplace in the back, and Mary Jo had carefully grown a garden at the edges.

Now Mary Jo went outside and shifted the water hose. The day had been hot and the grass was dry. She went around to the other side of the house where there was a sun cot and stretched out for a last exposure to the afternoon sun. Against the green of the cot she looked slim and delightfully curved in halter and shorts. Her auburn hair, cut short for the summer, caught glints in the sun, and the tan of her skin looked almost golden.

She had hardly settled down when she heard Bill clump down stairs and open the front screen door. This Saturday he had to work late. He would be on the job at six o'clock and would not be finished until two in the morning.

She sighed when she thought about it because there was a good show at the neighborhood theater, or they might have spent the evening with Carrie and Al. But as long as Bill worked for one of the news services they would have to resign themselves to changing hours. The local newspapers relied upon the wire services for news, and news around the world had no respect for hours.

Bill came out fully dressed, looking thin, tired, and stooped in his summer suit. He was in his early thirties and his hair was beginning to thin at the crown. He wore glasses with black frames, and he lacked the deep tan that his wife had acquired over weekends. He didn't particularly like the sun, he explained to people.

Mary Jo observed all of this with a glance and it made her conscious that although she was only three years his junior, she looked much younger. After five years of marriage she found it easier to make critical comparisons.

"You're not going, are you?" she asked, knowing that he was.

"Told Mac I'd relieve him a little early. He's taking the family down to the beach tonight. He has Monday off. Makes a good weekend for them."

"If you'll wait a few moments I'll get you something to eat. I just returned from the market."

"I fixed a sandwich while you were gone, and I'll eat later down there. This heat kills my appetite."

He lit a cigarette and came to the cot and solemnly regarded his wife.

"As they say, baby—you're really stacked. I wish it were my Saturday off."

She smiled up at him. "Listen to my lecherous husband! Do you want the car? I'm going to stay home."

"There's a good show at the Strand theater."

"I thought we might go tomorrow night. I'd rather see it with you."

"Good TV?"

"On a summer Saturday night? You know better. But there'll be something. Don't worry about me. I'll wait up. If it's still hot maybe we can take a ride. We can sleep in the morning."

She got up from the cot and walked with him to the car. He backed the Ford out and waved to her before he drove away. Idly she watched him turn a corner and then looked up and down the street. There was little activity. Across the street old Mrs. Tavish fussed with some flowers in her yard, and next door young Tommy McLain was mowing the lawn. He looked up and waved as he made a turn.

"Hi, Mrs. Camman!"

"Hi, Tommy. You need a power mower."

"Yeah. But try to talk Dad into it. He says when he was a kid he had twice the lawn to mow and didn't get paid for it." He grinned, the freckles on his face distorting cheerfully. "But I'm still getting paid!"

Mary Jo laughed and glanced up at the corner where the old rooming house constituted the only faintly undesirable place in the block. Fortunately, Mrs. Lindicott was strict about the roomers she took. She managed to keep an air of quiet respectability about the place, and, on the other hand, it was rather pleasant to have a few younger people in the neighborhood and some of Mrs. Lindicott's tenants were young.

One of them was going into the place now; a tall, blond young man who had the build of a lifeguard. He looked down the street toward Mary Jo as he went in, but he didn't smile nor nod. He seemed intent upon getting home, like a man just returning from work who is looking forward to a bath and some rest.

There still was a little late sun so Mary Jo went back to the sun cot. She had read somewhere that late afternoon sun had meagre tanning potentialities, but she liked the feel of it. There was something bordering upon the sensuous in the feel of warm sun, and Mary Jo relaxed and enjoyed it.

Sometimes the feeling she experienced when she was sun bathing reminded her of the summer she had spent at the beach when Cal Horlick had been there. And sometimes she wondered how it would have been if she had married Cal. She remembered the way he used to rub oil on her back and the lazy, drowsy effect his fingers had on her when they caressed and prodded her soft, pliant flesh.

And there was the night they had gone down on the beach in the moonlight. She wondered what Bill would say if she ever told him about that night. Bill was so desperately jealous. It would probably send him into a violent rage, or he would sulk for days, or he would question her incessantly as he had about the time she had gone for the car ride with Tab Mulane before she had married Bill.

Not that anything really had happened with Cal on the beach that night. As she remembered, she smiled to herself in the wisdom and knowledge of five years of marriage. Something could have happened if Cal had not been so terribly eager and excited. Too eager and excited, in fact. Afterward, he had been so ashamed and then, suddenly, the week was gone and he had left for school in the East and she had returned home.

There had been a few letters at first, but later on it didn't seem worth while for either of them to continue. Yet only an accident of nature might have made the difference between her not marrying Cal Horlick and marrying him. Or, for that matter, her coming to Bill a virgin, or not as a virgin.

Well, she had, and she supposed that was a small star in her crown for some reason or other, although she had never found anything too exciting about it with Bill. As a matter of fact, she had never felt as excited with Bill as she had that night with Cal— even if nothing really had happened with Cal.

She turned in the sun and listened to the whirr of the lawn mower next door and she supposed she should move the water hose again. Finally she slept and it was almost five o'clock when she awoke. She moved the hose, then went inside to fix dinner for herself.

The heat discouraged a hot meal so she prepared a fruit salad and a few cold cuts of meat and iced tea. She ate in the kitchen while she thumbed through a woman's magazine, noting ideas for interior decoration and studying the new fashions for autumn.

She had been born and reared in this city and had two older sisters who were married and lived in the East. Her father and mother lived across town, and her father was an auditor for one of the state's large lumber firms.

Sometimes she thought that her life had not been very exciting. She had been a rather plain looking girl in high school and at the state university. Later, as she became older, she acquired a slight maturity that strangely enhanced her natural prettiness. She had boyfriends and her most serious affair, until she met Bill, was with Cal Horlick, whom she had known most of her life. Even the serious moments of that affair had been restricted to the summer at the beach.

She met Bill Camman through the match-making of her long-time chum, Carrie, who had married Al Gould. Al worked on one of the newspapers and a new man named Bill Camman had come to town to work with one of the wire services. Carrie saw an opportunity to bring Mary Jo and Bill together and arranged a weekend for the two couples at the beach.

It had been a good outing. Mary Jo liked the thin, dark newsman from the midwest. They had much in common. They were both Methodists, they had belonged to Epworth Leagues, and had attended summer institutes. Bill talked about books and named ones she had liked, and they shared the same taste in music.

After the beach outing they dated steadily and after a time they went to fewer shows and parked frequently when he bought a used car. She was employed by that time at the insurance office and he frequently met her after work and they would have dinner downtown, or drive out to some place along a highway.

Thinking back upon it, Mary Jo supposed that their courtship probably had been identical with the courtships of thousands of other couples.

After the first few dates, marked by a certain politeness, reserve, and putting a best foot forward, the sparring had simmered down to a warm companionship and finally a first kiss and then the necking in a car, the holding of hands, the casual contact of bodies, the voicing of philosophies, beliefs, dreams and problems.

In those first days after the necking began, Mary Jo had been a little surprised and vaguely alarmed by the intensity of Bill's emotions, but she quickly learned to control them and restrict the kisses and love-making to definite limitations. Bill accepted these limitations without complaint or censure and he made no unreasonable demands to go beyond them, even if she vaguely wished at times that he would.

They saw quite a bit of Carrie and Al Gould, who adopted a manner of treating them as if they were virtually married, talking frequently about trips and projects the two couples could enjoy together "after you two are married."

Occasionally Carrie would ask Mary Jo pointblank if the date had been set; or she would build up Bill's qualities as a prospective husband and enthusiastically enumerate the many advantages of married life.

When Bill finally asked Mary Jo to marry him, it came as no surprise and seemed almost an incidental question. She had long since decided that they would eventually be married and subconsciously had begun to plan their life together.

They were married in a Methodist church and took a short honeymoon trip to San Francisco. They went by plane in a few hours and spent their first night at the Mark Hopkins Hotel.

In the privacy of their room they removed all the restraints and banished the frustrations and nurtured the excitements and passions of hours upon hours in a parked car and the living room of her parents' home after her folks had gone to bed.

The act of love proved to be a little painful and much more satisfactory than Mary Jo had been led to expect by the books she had read. And, as the months went by, Mary Jo quickly adapted herself to the role of being a wife with an intuitive knowledge that she had never expected too much of some things and that there was a good measure of happiness in others.

Mary Jo and Bill returned to their jobs and a program of saving so that they could buy a house. In the future there would be time for a family, but both of them wanted the house first and a feeling of permanency.

Mary Jo realized that Bill probably would never be a wealthy man, but he was a steady worker and his job with the news service offered them a good basic sense of security. The company had a generous retirement plan plus other fringe benefits. In the modern world of taxes and uncertainty, this was as much as most people could expect. If the news service should want to transfer

Bill to another city, he could probably find an equally good job on one of the local newspapers.

But occasionally—and only occasionally—she wondered about Cal Horlick. He had returned to the city and had practiced law for a few years and then had accepted a position in the district attorney's office. Once in a while she saw his name in a newspaper. He had not married and he led an active community life.

Once they had met on a downtown street—a studiously casual meeting with both attempting too hard to keep it casual.

When Mary Jo told Cal about her marriage, he nodded.

"I've met your husband. As a matter of fact, he's covered several cases I've handled and we sometimes have a cup of coffee together. You picked a good man, Mary Jo," he said with a smile.

"Haven't you found the right girl yet, Cal?"

"I think I did quite a while ago. Nothing came of it."

The implication was there, candidly and certain. It brought a quickening of Mary Jo's pulse and she knew that she blushed a little, but she also knew that she must ignore it. It was too late now. She loved Bill and they had a good married life together. There couldn't be anything else.

"You'll find another girl," she said lightly. "It's been so nice to see you, Cal."

"I must tell your husband that we're old school mates."

"He'll be interested."

They parted after a few incidental words and it was almost an hour before she felt the odd, aroused stirring in her blood subside.

Now on this late Saturday afternoon she thought about it and was vaguely annoyed.

"You're a respectable married woman," she scolded herself. "Behave yourself." And she managed a small, rueful laugh. One of these days Cal would be married to a girl from the social register up on the Heights and that would be that.

Mary Jo left the table, washed the few dishes she had used then called her mother. They chatted for the better part of an hour in the small and intimate talk of mother and daughter.

Afterwards she went outside again to move the hose and took a short stroll. The sun had gone down behind the Heights, but it still was quite light. When she returned to the house she sat on the porch until it was dusk.

Inside again, she went to the bedroom and turned on the light. Quickly she took off the halter and shorts and went into the bathroom where she took a lukewarm shower.

Returning to the bedroom, she stood nude before the long mirror and inspected her tan and the firm, slim, lines of her body. For a woman approaching thirty she showed not the slightest sign of a flabby muscle, nor a suspicious bulge. Her skin was smooth and clear. Her breasts were full and high and exquisitely rounded. There was a good firmness to her hips and thighs.

A slight breeze filtered through the screen of the open window and she stretched out on the bed luxuriating in its freshness and the sense of well being that filled her.

Suddenly she was glad that she had married Bill; that they had this house; and their plans and dreams and future before them. Perhaps Bill was not the most appealing or handsome man in the world, but he loved her and showed it in a thousand and one ways. She was lucky to have him. She could forego the excitements, the frenzied emotional upheaval that some other man might bring her for the steady security of Bill's gentleness, concern and devotion.

His faults were minor—the sudden jealousy that actually complimented her; his tendency to be untidy in his preoccupation about his job and his occasional attempts to write articles for magazines—articles that never sold for more than $50 or $100; and the other small faults that most women endure from a man.

Someday she would like to have his child and then there would be a fulfillment that would really cement their marital union.

She shut her eyes drowsily and thought that she must get up before the draft from the window brought her a summer cold, but she was comfortable and suddenly strangely happy. Perhaps she would nap for a few moments. She reached down and pulled the spread loose at the side and drew it over her.

Just before she dropped off into a deep sleep she worried vaguely about the unlocked doors downstairs.

CHAPTER THREE
BILL CAMMAN

Bill Camman checked the wire, glancing over the news stories that had been steadily unfolding from the chattering teletypes. There was the usual run of stories. Russia was on a new propaganda binge; a murder in Chicago; a fire in New York; the Senate was going to investigate government spending; a movie star had married again.

He rewrote several stories for the radio wire, getting them ready to be sent to radio stations that subscribed to the news service.

He worked quickly and steadily until he struck a lull and decided to go out for dinner. He left the building and went to a corner café where most of the newsmen ate.

He ordered ham and eggs and read a magazine while he ate, glancing over the book reviews and personality briefs. When he had finished eating he put down the magazine and had his second cup of coffee.

Sometimes hot weather brought him a touch of nostalgia for North Dakota and the wheat country where he had been born and reared. He remembered the summer heat, the wheat ripening in the sun, the dust following a rancher's car along a dirt feeder road, the brassy shimmer of the sun upon the land.

Most of his early years had been spent in a small town in the Northwest corner of the state near the Canadian border and the

Montana state line. His father had published the small weekly newspaper there, making a precarious living for a large family. He had died when Bill was a senior at the university.

Bill had gone home for the funeral and an older brother had taken over the newspaper and given a home to the mother. Bill had returned to finish school and to take a job on a Duluth newspaper, and eventually with the news service.

Sipping at the hot coffee, he thought about it now; the way his life had worked out; and the way it might possibly work out for the future.

His marriage with Mary Jo was, of course, the big turning point. Until then he had dreamed a little of a foreign correspondent's berth with the service, or perhaps a spot in New York. He could picture himself—in those earlier days—as a feature writer for a national magazine; an authority on foreign events; the head of a bureau. His ambitions were a trifle vague, but drove him with spasmodic industry at times.

Meeting Mary Jo and falling in love with her had changed most of that. Now he thought more about eventually heading the bureau in this city, or of leaving the news service and building himself a place on one of the local newspapers.

Buying their home, fixing it up, and planning for the future had changed his evaluation of things. Eventually they would probably have one or two kids. He'd become a man of some stature in the community. Perhaps someday he might write a book.

Some of the men made a few extra dollars occasionally covering crime stories for the national "true crime" magazines. He might begin there. He would have access to the stories when they broke. It might be a better means of breaking into the important magazine market than the occasional trade journal stories that he wrote.

The main thing, of course, was his life with Mary Jo. He wished he could have stayed home this Saturday night. Perhaps they could have gone over to Al and Carrie's for some cards and a few glasses of beer. Afterwards they would come home and he would take Mary Jo to bed.

He smiled and sipped at the coffee again. Well, she was going to wait up for him and they'd have something to eat when he got home, and perhaps she'd be in the mood, anyhow. It was something to look forward to on a dull Saturday night at the office.

Max Sinto, a desk man on the morning paper, came in and greeted him. He sat down beside Bill, glanced at Bill's empty plate, and said, "Ham and eggs?"

Bill nodded.

"I'll have some of the same," Max decided. He was a short, fat, tired looking man in his forties. "Quiet night. Always quiet on Saturday night, it seems. I wish I could go home."

"Saturday night blues," Bill grinned. "Anything doing locally?"

"A little crime. The city is growing up into a big boy on the crime statistics list."

"Crime's increasing everywhere. I saw an FBI report the other day. Makes you wonder."

"A lot of kids are growing up into psychos," Max said decisively. "It's the educational system. Or the parents. Homes aren't what they used to be."

"Or the nuclear age, the economy of the nation, mass communication, automobiles, or satellites," Bill smiled. "Who knows?"

"Yeah. How's the wife?"

"Swell. Bitching a little because she doesn't like my Saturday night stints, but not too much. She knew about newsmen before she married me."

A waitress took Sinto's order and Bill asked for more coffee. It suddenly had occurred to him that Sinto sometimes sold a true crime story. Maybe he could learn a few of the angles from the chubby newsman.

"How's the crime-writing business these days?" he asked. "Sold anything lately?"

Sinto shook his head. "I'm too tired when I get home to write anything. Guess I'm getting old. Besides, I haven't run across anything extra good for a while. Most of the murders lately have been cut and dried. No sex angles, no chase, no big mystery."

"They like a sex angle, don't they?"

"Who doesn't, boy? Sex is what makes the world go round." He grinned. "My world's been turning pretty slow lately. I guess I *am* getting old. My wife says all I want to do is go to sleep reading a book."

"There have been some rape cases lately," Bill suggested. "Will they go for those?"

"There has to be more than just ordinary rape, I think. Hell, that's getting too common. Have you noticed the crime statistics? Around twenty thousand cases reported every year, and when you consider the ones that aren't reported, it really runs into figures."

"I suppose there are a lot that are never reported."

"No one will ever know, but they tell me it's the exception when one is reported. Women are afraid their names will get in the news; or afraid of their husbands, or families, or friends and neighbors. You can't blame them, in a way, if they never tell anyone that they've had it."

"Then you look for murder cases for the mags?"

"Those and sensational robberies, bank stick-ups, chases— all the stuff that makes headlines and has drama. Why? You thinking of trying some stories?"

"Maybe. If I'm not stepping on your toes."

"Hell, I'm not stringing for any of those magazines. Go ahead. Maybe I can help you."

"You usually try to get an assignment, don't you?"

"As soon as a case breaks and I think I want to cover it for one of the books, I wire for an assignment. If I get the go-ahead, I've a good chance of selling the story."

"Maybe I'll try one. If I spot a good one."

"You guys on the wire are in a spot to get them," Sinto said. "You cover the state."

"Do the cops cooperate?"

"Sure. Most of them hope for a little publicity. You usually get good cooperation from the D.A.s, too. Horlick works most of the crime stuff here."

"I know him. Nice guy."

"He'll serve a couple of years as assistant and then try for the D.A. job when old man Crowther retires. Probably get it, too. He's smart."

Sinto decided to have a beer before he ate and ordered it.

"Had your vacation yet?" he asked Bill.

"Mary Jo doesn't get one until September. We may take a week at the beach, and another working on the house."

"You two have really put in a lot of work on that old place."

"And dough," Bill grinned. "But it's been cheaper than buying a new place, and we've lots of room."

"It's okay if you get it fixed up. We've got an old place and all my wife talks about is looking for a new one. We've had enough of worn out plumbing and leaky roofs to last us a lifetime. But it takes dough to buy a new one these days."

They talked a while longer and Bill left and returned to the newsroom. He checked the wires again. Nothing important had come in while he was eating, so he put his feet on a desk and thought about his conversation with Max Sinto.

Maybe a good murder case would break and he could get a quick assignment to cover it for a magazine. It could work into a pretty fair sideline, and the pay was reasonably good. With a few breaks they could buy a new car and fix up the rumpus room in the basement.

Lately Mary Jo had been talking about hi-fi. Maybe they could get into that, too, and run a few speakers around the place. It would be nice to have one out on the patio, and one in the bedroom.

Mary Jo liked Mantovani. That would be a nice deal. Put on a stack of Mantovani mood music before they went to bed. Mary Jo might like that. He'd like it himself. A couple ought to really enjoy life a little, build things up for their moments, make the most of what they had.

It might be a good idea, too, if he cultivated his friendship with Cal Horlick. It could prove useful if a murder story broke and there was a chance to cover it for one of the magazines. A friend in the D.A.'s office could be a big help.

The bell on a teletype rang a bulletin signal and he got up and looked at the words as they rattled from the machine. A tornado had ripped through a southern village. Well, at least he didn't have to worry about that out here on the West Coast.

It was hot in the office. He'd be glad when he could leave. He'd go home and Mary Jo would fix them something to eat. They might even take a short ride in the coolness of the night.

Tomorrow he could do a few things around the house. He'd better remember to put a new gasket on the shower control. It dripped hot water, and since they had bought the house they had learned that it cost money to heat water.

He went to the machines and tore off the long tapes to work over the stories.

He had no way of knowing that at that moment Mary Jo left the bathroom at their home and reminded herself to tell Bill about the leaky faucet. She walked nude into the bedroom unaware that across the street a man watched her through a pair of Japanese binoculars stolen from a department store.

CHAPTER FOUR
MILES SALIN

M iles Salin had intended to take a bath as soon as he got home from work that Saturday afternoon, but there was only one bathroom on the floor and it was in use. He knew that the occupant was Thelma Jorgson because she had left her room door ajar.

He heard the sound of running water in the shower. It would be another ten or fifteen minutes before she would finish. Of course, he could go downstairs and use the shower on the first floor, and there was another in the basement, but he preferred the one near his room. Meanwhile, at least he could get out of his work clothes and into a pair of blues and a T-shirt.

The room was hot so he left the door open to get some cross ventilation. He glanced out the window as he opened it and looked at the yard across the street. The girl was on the sun cot. She wore a halter and shorts. A few moments before he had seen her out at the curb as she watched her husband drive away. This was the night that he worked late. This was the night of the plan, and a hot knot of excitement began to squeeze his insides.

His gaze moved slowly over the woman's legs and hips and breasts. Her skin would be tan and warm and very white where the tan ended. She would be soft and pliable and vibrant. He let his imagination play with her as he watched her from across the few intervening yards, and he was startled when he heard Thelma Jorgson speak behind him.

"Day dreaming?"

He turned to find her lounging in the doorway wearing a rayon robe. Her face looked soap-clean and her hair was slightly damp and curly. Obviously she wore nothing under the robe and he was uncomfortably aware of the feminine curves and depressions to which the rayon molded itself.

He forced a casual smile and said, "It's been a hot day. Just getting some air. My room's stuffy."

"It must have been awful at the lot today. I was shopping and passed it this afternoon. You were busy, and there isn't a speck of shade."

"You get used to it."

"Well, I don't want to disturb you, but I need some advice and I thought you could help me."

He wished she would get her advice elsewhere, but he couldn't be rude to her. He couldn't risk antagonizing anyone.

"Sure," he said.

Thelma came in without his asking and closed the door behind her. She sat in a rocking chair across the room from his bed and arranged the drape of her robe to cover her legs. She did it primly and carefully as if she were very conscious of her body.

"I'm thinking of buying a used car," she explained. "Perhaps you could tell me what kind to look for. You know so much about them and I'm completely lost trying to decide."

He sat on his bed and wondered if she really wanted to buy a car or if she was looking for an excuse to come into his room. Maybe he could go right ahead and stand up and pull her to her feet and kiss her. She wasn't wearing anything under that robe, and she had closed the door after her.

But he couldn't. He wanted no involvement with a woman living next door to him. Sure! She'd get what she probably wanted and then they'd start spending their nights together and she'd probably get pregnant and he'd be in a jam. He wanted none of that. He wanted no woman to have a hold on him; no woman to support; no woman to whom he had to answer.

"It all depends on how much you want to spend," he said.

"Could I get anything worth while for around five hundred dollars?"

"You could get a pretty good car for that. Maybe a Chevvy or a Ford."

"Doctor drives a Ford for his house calls. Mrs. Mont— that's Doctor's wife—usually drives their Cadillac. Doctor always praises his Ford."

"They're good cars. A Chevvy is good—and so is a Plymouth. You can't go far wrong. The main thing is to find a car that has had good care."

"But how do I find a car like that?"

"Well, some of the used car dealers are honest enough." He named a few.

"I thought you might know someone who keeps his car at the lot and wants to sell it."

"Not offhand. But I'll ask around."

"I thought, too, that maybe you'd look a car over for me before I bought it. You could tell if it had been in a wreck or anything."

"I'll be glad to."

She smiled her thanks. "I knew you could help."

"Just let me know."

She smiled again and glanced around his room. "You need a few pictures in here."

"I used to fool around with photography," he told her. "I thought maybe I'd blow up some scenes when I get a chance to use a darkroom again."

"Did you know there's one in the basement? Before Mr. Lindicott died photography was his hobby. He showed me the darkroom once. Mrs. Lindicott would probably let you use it."

Thelma awakened a genuine spark of interest in him this time. In high school he had found a great deal of enjoyment in the hobby, and at one time or another he had obtained a large assortment of candid shots of girls on the beach near his home. Perhaps with the new extremely fast film and a telescopic lens he might get pictures of the bedroom across the street, especially when the overhead light was on.

"I don't suppose Mrs. Lindicott would mind," he said thoughtfully.

"Then you'd have something to do evenings instead of staying in this stuffy room," Thelma murmured. "Don't you have a girl?"

"They don't interest me much," he said carefully, smiling to avoid slighting her. "I guess I haven't thought much about them."

"Maybe it's time you should! Some dates would probably be good for you. You're much too nice to be wasting your time in a stuffy room, or even in a darkroom, for that matter!"

She was not being subtle about it, Miles thought. And now the robe had parted a little so that he could see the smooth whiteness of one leg up to her knee. She must know that he had looked, and she hadn't covered her leg again.

If she knew what he planned for the night she wouldn't be deliberately tempting him to make a pass at her, or to ask her for a date. Or maybe she'd like to do what he wanted to do. But it couldn't be that way. She would have a hold on him afterwards.

"I guess I'm just the shy type," he said with a grin. "You let me know if you want me to look over a car for you. I can ask one of the mechanics I know to check it over." He stood expectantly and looked down at her. "Just let me know," he said again.

With a slight expression of disappointment she rose and went to the door. "I hope you don't mind my asking," she said.

"You're just being smart," he assured her. "Too many people buy lemons because they don't ask questions and get help."

Miles opened the door for her and stood there while she went out, feeling the slight brush of her body against him as she passed, and smelling the soapy cleanliness of her. For a brief second he was tempted to grab her and pull her against him. He drew back a trifle and the impulse was gone. It was too dangerous.

She walked to her own door, thanked him again, then went inside and closed the door softly after her. In a few moments he heard her radio playing.

"She probably would," he told himself, a shine of sweat appearing on his forehead. "She'd probably like it. But she's not for me. I've got better pickings. Tonight!"

Miles picked up a towel and his shaving equipment and locked himself in the bathroom. He shaved carefully, then took a hot shower and followed it with a cold one. He rubbed himself down briskly with a rough bath towel and then used a few drops of face lotion, enjoying its sting. He felt set-up now. He felt ready and there was a buoyant high tone to his body, a rich, heady sense of excitement vibrating along his nerves.

Back in his room he locked his door and took his recent purchases from the dresser drawer.

He unrolled about three inches of the wide adhesive tape, cut it with scissors, and stuck the short strip back on the roll.

He unrolled a length of bandage and cut it, slit it down the middle at one end, then carefully rolled the strip back on the rest of the roll so that the split end would be ready for tying when the bandage was unwound and applied.

He brought out the top of the woman's stocking that he had cut and pulled it over his head. He had cut two eye holes, although he could almost see well enough through the thin material when it was close to his face. The top of the stocking made an excellent hood. He took it off and put it in the dresser drawer.

He brought out the short lengths of rope and tied slip nooses in one end of each, carefully rolled each length, and placed them beside the other things on the dresser.

In the next room the radio suddenly became silent. A moment later Miles heard Thelma's door close and her quick walk as she passed his room and went down the stairs. The front screen door slammed. She probably was going to a movie alone, he thought. There had been almost a frustrated wrath in the sound of her footsteps.

He went to the window and peered out. It was dusk and there was a light in the kitchen of the house across the street. He pulled a chair to the window and sat down to wait.

When the light went on in the bedroom across the street he got the binoculars and watched. He saw the woman take off her shorts and bra and leave the room. He guessed that she had gone into the bathroom. After a time she returned and stood in front of the long mirror as if she was admiring herself.

Miles' blood began to pound in his chest and temples and he adjusted the glasses finely. His breathing turned ragged and uneven as he watched her stretch languidly on the bed; and noticed the drowsy way in which she pulled the spread over her. She had left the overhead light on, but he was certain that she was asleep.

This was earlier than he had anticipated. It would be better to wait at least another hour or so. She probably would sleep. She often did during the early hours of a Saturday night when she was alone.

There was one thing more to do. He left the window and from another drawer in the dresser he brought out a short, thick cylinder of polished steel that he had found in the scrap pile of the garage next to the parking lot. It was about four inches long with a small hole drilled through one end. From the same drawer he brought a short section of leather thong and a roll of electrician's tape.

Working quickly, Miles taped the length of steel with several layers and then tied a loop through the hole at the end of the cylinder so that the thong would slip over his wrist. He tested the loop and the weight of the steel in his hand. It made a heavy, deadly weapon—a home-made blackjack that could easily crush a skull, break a jaw or fracture a shoulder.

Now it was time to dress.

Quickly he got out of his blues, T-shirt and shorts. He stepped into the coveralls and zipped them up the front. The new cloth felt a trifle stiff against his skin and he stood back to look at the fit. The legs were long and he turned up the bottoms into neat cuffs. Then he carefully distributed the items from the dresser top to pockets in his single garment.

From a closet he brought a lightweight jacket and put it on. He was satisfied. It looked as if he wore slacks, sport shirt and jacket. That would certainly be the description anyone who might see him in the dark of the street would pass along.

He wore slip-on loafers with crepe soles and his footsteps were only a whisper as he walked to his door, unlocked it, and opened it to listen.

The house was quiet except for the small radio in Mrs. Lindicott's kitchen. He could leave without being observed. Closing his door behind him, Miles went down the stairs, softly closed the front screen door as he left the house, and paused to look around. No one was on the street and the heavy tree branches darkened the sidewalks and pavement.

He crossed the street and followed a hedge that separated the old house from the next home. The back yard was dark, and he stepped to the back porch where he slipped out of the jacket and hid it beneath a shrub.

Taking the hood from a pocket, he pulled it over his crew-cut hair and down over his face, adjusting the holes for his eyes. Finally he put on the lightweight gloves.

He was certain that the back door would not be barred, and he found only a screen door barring his entrance. It was unlocked, and he went inside and crossed the darkened kitchen into a short hallway and to the stairs.

The first step creaked with his weight and he froze for a few seconds, listening, looking up the stairway. The bedroom door was open and the overhead light was reflected dimly down the stairs. No sound came from above as he started the ascent, putting his feet down close to the edge of each step to lessen the possibility of more creaking.

He gained the landing and without pausing he stepped to the open bedroom door and looked in. The woman still slept though she had moved in her sleep so that she was on one side with her back to the doorway. The spread covered her to her shoulders, and one arm was beneath her, the other resting on the pillow where she rested half-face down.

Silently Miles took the bandage from his pocket, and the adhesive tape. He pulled the short strip of tape loose and crept forward.

At the bedside he quietly stuck a corner of the tape to the edge of the headboard and put the roll of bandage in a breast pocket of the coveralls. The woman slept quietly as Miles left the side of the bed and went to a light switch by the doorway.

He flipped the switch. There was a slight click and the room became dark except for the dim light that came through the open window. He held his breath and waited, a claw of tension stirring his vitals. The woman continued to breathe evenly in her deep sleep. He stepped out of the loafers, moved to the bed again and looked down at her, waiting for his eyes to become accustomed to the dim light. Miles knew exactly what he would do, exactly how he would use his hands—the tape, the bandage, the ropes. His breathing became tight. A rough surge of feeling rocketed through him, almost scalding in its intensity.

Taking the tape from the edge of the headboard, he cupped it, sticky side out, in the palm of his left hand. Slowly and with a slight tremor the hand crept forward toward the woman's mouth until it was poised directly over it. He took a deep, soft breath and the excitement churning inside him became painfully sharp.

Miles' muscles tensed, then he moved in a fast, coordinated sequence of actions. The cupped hand clamped over the mouth of the sleeping woman and the adhesive tape sealed her mouth. At the same instant he swung his left leg over his victim so that he straddled her with his weight as he half knelt above her and forced her body over and face down.

She struggled in a frantic awakening and he gripped her hard between his knees. One hand brought out the roll of bandage and he shifted higher until his knees pinned down her flailing arms.

Quickly he slipped the bandage across her eyes and unwound it and tied it so that she was firmly blindfolded.

He turned her so that her back was against the bed and then brought out the short lengths of rope. He slipped a noose over one wrist, then leaned forward to tie the other end near a bed caster.

She had stopped struggling now and he heard her breathing heavily through her nostrils.

When he finished with the ropes he pulled down the blind at the window and turned on a bed lamp. He retreated from the bed and took off the hood. His fingers trembled as he sought the zipper on the coveralls and pulled it down and kicked out of the garment.

He looked down at the trussed woman and his mouth was dry and parched while a heavy thrumming sensation pounded all through his body.

This was exactly as he had planned it.

CHAPTER FIVE
GEORGE MARTIN

Detective Lieutenant George Martin listened attentively to Bill Camman's emotion-tinged voice. They sat in the kitchen of the old house and the pre-dawn light of early morning almost made the overhead light unnecessary. Camman had fixed instant coffee for them as soon as they had returned from the hospital where Mary Jo was sleeping under sedation.

Upstairs in the bedroom one of the laboratory men still worked with fingerprint powder and the other tools of his job. Outside two uniformed men took advantage of the early light to make a more thorough search of the yard and a close inspection of the porch.

Martin did not think that they would find much. The attack had been too well planned. The pre-cut rope, the tape, the bandage, and the method precluded much chance that there would be fingerprints or other tangible evidence.

The rope might be traced, but the adhesive tape was like tape sold over dozens of store counters every day, as was the bandage. Whoever had done this had planned carefully.

Mary Jo Camman had tried to fill in details, but she was still a little hysterical when Martin had seen her at the hospital, and she had been blindfolded almost from the first moment of the attack. She could give no definite description—just that she knew he had been a large man because of his weight and strength; that his voice had sounded young. The voice actually was all she had to cling to for an identification, and even that was only a memory of a voice tense with excitement and passion; a voice that uttered obscenities and threats and—strangely—endearments at times.

The doctor had given her a sedative and suggested that further questioning be delayed until the next day.

"She'll be all right," he assured them. "This is shock, but she hasn't been physically hurt. Her lips will be sore from his tearing off the tape and replacing it, and her wrists and ankles are chafed from her struggling against the ropes. But that's all."

"All!" Camman protested. "She's been—" He stopped speaking suddenly and stared at the doctor, a peculiar look of anguish on his face.

"He might have killed her," the doctor said quietly. "Rape and murder go hand in hand more often than you'd suspect. Lieutenant Martin will confirm that." He glanced at Martin.

"That's right, Camman," Martin said, his expression serious and intent. "From what the doctor says we'd better let her sleep now. I'd like to go out to the house with you now."

Camman nodded, and they left the hospital. Camman had his car and led the way. He swung into the driveway and parked. Martin parked the police car at the curb behind one that already had been dispatched to the house. Two officers sat in it waiting. He spoke to them quietly and met Camman at the front door.

Camman switched on lights and nodded toward the stairs. "Up there," he said. "I'll show you."

Martin carefully inspected the bedroom from the doorway. He saw the four ropes still tied to the caster fittings, a rope at each corner with the empty slip nooses at the ends. He saw the disorder of the night spread on the bed, the dried stains, the pillow on the floor. At the side of the bed on the floor was a wrinkled strip of bandage and a small length of moist-looking adhesive tape.

"What time did you get home?" Martin asked.

"At a little after two. I thought my wife was asleep and came up to ask her if she wanted to go for a ride."

"And you found her tied on the bed?"

Camman nodded mutely, his eyes dark with misery. After a few seconds he said, "Her eyes were bandaged so that she couldn't see, and her mouth was covered with adhesive tape." He turned back to the stairs, running his fingers nervously through his hair. "I'm going to fix some coffee," he said. "I can't think straight."

Martin went down with him and called in the uniformed men and gave them orders. He used the telephone in the hallway to call for help from the laboratory, then went out to the kitchen where he sat at a table with Camman and sipped at the hot coffee the newspaperman had prepared.

"You have absolutely no idea who might have done it?" he asked.

"I told you. I haven't. Who'd do a thing like that? Who'd plan it so carefully?" Bill's voice was filled with anguish.

"Someone who's had an eye on her for quite a while, I think," Martin said. "It's too well planned to be something impulsive."

"Look, Lieutenant … have there been other cases like this?"

"Not reported. At least, not in this city. Not with ropes, bandages and tape gimmicks. Usually it's a back seat of a car, or a prowler and rapist coming through a window. Not anything as elaborate as this. Have you noticed anyone watching her?"

"No."

"I'll have men cover the neighborhood tomorrow."

"Will it do any good?" Camman demanded grimly.

"I don't know. Someone may have seen something. Someone may live in the neighborhood who's been watching her."

"I doubt it. Not in this neighborhood. They're all old time residents, except the rooming house up on the corner."

"Maybe there, then. We'll check it out tomorrow. And maybe the lab will find something. One fingerprint would help."

"If he planned that well, he probably wore gloves."

"Probably."

Camman finished his coffee and got up and made more, strong and black.

"I don't have to ask you to keep this as quiet as possible," he said to the detective. "You understand that."

"You're a newspaperman. You know the papers here won't use it, and I'll keep it as quiet as I can."

"My wife didn't want me to report it."

"Most of them don't."

"But if you don't catch up with him, he could get some other woman. He could come back here again. We'd be frightened from here on out. Afraid for her to be alone. We'd be living behind locked doors."

"We'd get more like him if they were reported. But a woman's usually in shock, and ashamed, and—well it's something a woman doesn't want to talk about or think about."

"I'd kill him if I could find him." Camman's features were red and swollen with rage and his eyes had a narrow, ugly look about them.

"You have a right to feel that way, but you wouldn't. You know it's our job to handle it."

"I suppose so."

"If we catch up with him, your wife will have to testify. What about that? Do you think she will?"

"Not if it's public."

"We could arrange it otherwise."

"Then I think she would. I hope so."

"I want her to think about everyone you know, or have met recently, or who has been around here," Martin added. "I want to screen them. Any salesmen. Strangers hanging around the neighborhood. Anyone she thought might have been following her."

"I don't know how much she can help you. We'll have to wait until tomorrow. I can't help you any with that stuff. I wish I could, but I haven't noticed anyone … and I can't think any of our friends who would do anything like this."

"Maybe your wife can give us a lead. I hope so. We'll need every lead we can get."

Bill sat down at the table again and thoughtfully lit a cigarette. "Tonight at dinner I was talking about rape and murders with Max Sinto. He's on the desk at the Sentinel."

"I know him," Martin nodded. "He occasionally does a true crime job for one of the magazines."

"When I was talking with him, rape or murder seemed a long way off. It didn't occur to me that I would be face to face with one of them in my own home within a few hours. I guess we figure everything can happen to the other guy, but not to us."

"And then it does," the detective said.

"It can change your whole life," said Bill, scrubbing his perspiring face with the palm of one hand.

The detective looked at him solemnly. "Listen, Bill … it doesn't have to be that bad. Your wife is alive. She'll be all right by tomorrow. Don't let this throw you."

The newspaperman didn't look up, but kept his eyes focused on his coffee cup. "That's right," he said. "But I still think I'd kill the guy."

"Okay. As long as you don't try to do it. Try to take it a little easy for a few days. Let it get straightened out in your mind. And just remember that she's alive—that you didn't find her with her face battered in, dead, mutilated."

Martin got up and rinsed his cup and put it on the drainboard. "You'd better get some sleep. I just heard the lab man come down, so he's probably finished for the time being. But don't clean up that room, or go in there. We may want another look after we've talked with your wife."

He went outside, conferred with the uniformed men and then with the lab man. None of them had turned up anything important.

"We'll check out the rope," the lab man said. "It probably came from one of the dime stores. That may give us a lead. The guy probably wore gloves when he touched anything that would pick up a print."

Martin nodded and got in his car. In a little while his night would be finished and he'd be going home. He wondered exactly how he'd feel if he found Alice tied to a bed with her eyes blindfolded and her mouth silenced by tape. He'd probably want to kill as much as Bill Camman did.

That usually was the husband's reaction, but later on it was sometimes different, he mused. Some men take a thing like that with a lot of common sense, but others brood about it. He remembered husbands who apparently held their wives somehow responsible for what had happened. Sometimes, perhaps, with justification. Wives going home from bars with strange men. Wives getting a kick out of mild flirtations that suddenly got out of hand. But even with the others there sometimes was a strange look of accusation in a husband's eyes, and a bewildered, hurt look in the wife's.

How did any man know exactly how he'd feel about it? How would he feel about Alice? But it wasn't likely to happen with Alice. Not with two boys in high school in the same house; and both boys on the high school football eleven. Suddenly he felt a warmth of satisfaction in thinking about his sons and his family life. A man had reason to be a little proud when he had a family like that!

He drove toward headquarters in the early morning traffic and thought about the night's events. Earlier there had been the stick-up at the gas station; then one of his men had brought in a small, dark man who was pushing reefers to high school kids on a corner; and then the Camman case.

He remembered abruptly that this was a short change in hours for him. He'd filled in on the late tour because of vacation schedules, and he was due back on the day tour this morning. No one would expect him to show up until later in the day. A man was entitled to a few hours of sleep, but he'd have to follow through with the Camman woman. They probably wouldn't let him talk to her until noon or later. The sedation had been heavy.

As he parked in the lot in back of the station house he again remembered the look on Bill Camman's face.

"That guy isn't taking it easy," he told himself. "His wife may have trouble with him before it's over."

CHAPTER SIX
MARY JO

There was no need for her to stay in this hospital bed. It was almost one o'clock and she should get up and leave. She felt tired and her body was sore in places; her arms and legs from straining against the ropes; her wrists and ankles from chafing against the bonds that had held her; and her bruised and swollen mouth from the adhesive tape.

A nurse had brought her lunch and smiled enigmatically when Mary Jo asked when she could leave.

"The doctor will be here shortly after lunch," the nurse replied. "He'll probably let you go then. Your husband was here for about an hour, but you were still sleeping."

The food was tasteless to her, but Mary Jo ate it knowing that it would help to drive away the washed-out feeling of exhaustion; give her strength to combat the vivid memory of what had happened to her a few hours before.

There was no way to run away from what had occurred; no way to erase it, to forget it, to ignore it. She had read about people who had mental lapses, or who somehow did manage to erase a memory, but this was not for her. As long as she lived she would remember in detail the things that had happened.

And in the innermost core of her mind there would always be the secret shame that her body had betrayed her. This was the thing that she must try hardest to forget. If anything could possibly be erased from her memory, this was it.

"Not at first," she thought, recalling the terror that had given her frantic strength in the first few moments. She shuddered as she recalled her abrupt awakening, and the frantic effort to escape in the darkness—to tear free from the strong hands, to cry out against the sealing tape over her mouth, to see against the encompassing pressure of the cloth shielding her eyes.

She had fought with every ounce of her strength, but the attacking weight and strength had been too much. There had been the rasp of the rope on her right wrist and heavy movement over her, and then the arm was secured and she hurt it trying to free it. A quick prying movement had pinioned her other arm flat so that she was on her back and the man straddled her and his weight left her for a second as he pulled the rope tight and she lay with arms outstretched.

She had kicked desperately and futilely to avoid the hands that grasped at her ankles. But inevitably there came the binding stricture of the tight noose over the left ankle, and the right, and the anchoring of the ropes so that her legs had a little freedom that was brought up short by the pull-back restraint of the ropes.

Suddenly she had experienced an utter futility of defeat and her body had become quiet while her heart beat madly and she heard surreptitious movement in the blackness about her.

She tried to breathe deeply through her nose, feeling a suffocation from her taped mouth and wanting great gulps of air in her lungs. After a few seconds she managed to breathe easier and she felt a tingle of expectation creep over her skin as if it awaited pain or the touch of undefined sensations.

She recoiled violently from the first touch of hands that moved over her shoulders—hands that touched lightly and softly and intimately. And so the horrible nightmare began.

It was a frantic nightmare that was, at the same time, an agony of sensation because she knew that it was reality. Sometime in the nightmare her body had overpowered her mind beneath the relentlessly caressing hands of her attacker and the insidious touch of his lips and tongue.

Time became a strange eternity of helpless sensation and a great weakness washed over her. The last resistance ebbed from her because she could not fight it, and the caressing took new forms and patterns and insinuated itself into her consciousness until she felt her breathing become hard and each futile movement of her body to pull away, or avoid, or resist became an accomplice to the caress.

The insidious, tormenting play of the man's hands and mouth sent an ecstatic, burning fever, such as she had never known before, rioting through her blood.

Finally she felt movement above her and the shifting of weight on the mattress and her complete defenselessness somehow increased the frenzy within her so that she was betrayed again and yielded to her attacker rather than obeying her impassioned determination to withdraw.

A hand had ripped the tape from her lips and a heavy, moist mouth ground softly against hers. A single, despairing moan came from her throat and one desperate effort to will the urgency to stop, and then a sudden surrender that was violent and as self-consuming as a searing burst of flame.

Afterwards there had been the shame and confusion and the tears that struggled to release themselves against the binding cloth. There was the heart-sick revulsion when he returned, and this time it was different and rough and her body twisted in anguish until a numbness enveloped her and she escaped from reality into a nightmare of blackness and helpless submission.

So, in the hospital bed, she let herself remember in detail. She lived again the long—endlessly long—wait until he was suddenly gone, the listening for the car as Bill arrived, his footsteps on the stairs, his voice.

Eventually the wait was over and then hysteria bore down upon her, and she knew only Bill's presence, of going to the bathroom and the nausea that followed—racking sobs that wrenched her strength completely away from her then falling into endless darkness; of water on her face; of being carried to the car and the smell of a hospital.

She walked numbly down a hospital corridor with Bill grasping her arm firmly and helping her to stand erect. They entered a room where white enamel shone in a very white light and finally a nurse spoke soothingly and a doctor came and spoke to her.

This thing had happened to other women, and now it had happened to her. It was a terrible shock to realize that the body had accepted the rape and dismissed it functionally, but not the mind. The scar was there in her memory, everlastingly colored by shame and confusion. This must be a secret never shared, never told, but to remain with her throughout the rest of her life.

The doctor came into the room briskly. He was middle-aged and heavy-set. His eyes were kindly and he smiled as he came to the bed and automatically felt for a pulse.

"All right?" he asked.

"I think so," she whispered.

He nodded and inspected her wrists and looked at her mouth. "Your husband can take you home any time."

She avoided his eyes momentarily and let a feminine practicality dictate her thinking. There was a question to ask.

"Doctor … what if there's a pregnancy?"

"It's a remote chance. I wouldn't worry about it."

"Could something be done legally if it did happen?"

"Let's worry if it happens. I doubt very much that it will. If you have any reason later to think that you are pregnant, either see me or see your family doctor and have him call me."

He stood back from the bed and glanced toward the closed door. "There's a detective waiting out there to talk with you. Feel up to it?"

"I can't tell him much. The same one I talked to last night?"

The doctor nodded. "Anything may help. You'll have to see him sooner or later. Now might be better, while it's fresh in your mind."

"Won't it always be fresh in my mind, doctor? Do you ever completely forget a thing like this?" There was a strange, breathless note in her voice.

"You can be sensible about it," he replied. "It's done. That can't be changed. But you weren't permanently injured. Remember that."

"I'll try, Doctor."

The doctor opened the door and brought in the detective and introduced him as Lieutenant Martin. He looked as if he might be an insurance agent, or a moderately successful attorney, or the owner of a small business. He had his hat off and he wore a banker's gray suit with a white collar and a subdued gray tie.

"I didn't talk with you much last night, Mrs. Camman," he said quietly. "But your husband and I had a long talk, and we went out to your place. I hope you feel well enough to answer a few questions now."

"The doctor assures me that I'm perfectly sound physically," Mary Jo said, a little bitterly, looking toward the doorway through which the doctor had left. "I'm all right. I've only been raped." There was almost a vicious satisfaction in admitting the fact coldly and in plain words. This couldn't happen to a man. It was a man's world.

The detective sensed her frustration and looked away from her for a second. If she wanted to display anger and outrage, it was her right, and now was as good a time as any. When she said no more, he looked at her again.

"We want to get him," he said. "Maybe you can help."

"Not much. I was asleep when he attacked me. He had turned out the light. I couldn't see him … only feel his hands and hear his breathing … and later his voice."

"You said last night that you think he's young and fairly large."

"Yes." She was sure of this because she remembered his strength compared with Bill's, the different feel of arms crushing her close, of larger hands, of greater weight. "He was larger than Bill."

"You said his voice sounded young. What did he say?"

"He—he made love to me. Called me beautiful, wonderful … the words men use. Later—when he became more excited—he used other words … obscenities. The second time he was harsh and he was rough with me."

"There were two times?"

"Yes."

"The first time he was not rough?"

"No. He took a long time. He—well, he did things to me first."

"Did he hurt you?"

"No. Nothing like that. He was gentle … almost careful not to hurt me." Her voice sounded shocked and hushed to her own ears.

"Was there anything that may have reminded you of someone?" Martin asked.

"Absolutely nothing."

"Do you think you would recognize his voice?"

"I'm not sure. He kept it very low."

"Did you hear him do anything around the room? Open drawers or make some sound that indicated he touched anything? We've dusted the room for prints and found nothing unusual. Perhaps we missed some place."

Mary Jo thought a moment, then said, "He pulled down the blind and then he turned on the bedlamp. That's all I remember about his movements away from me."

"When he left?"

"Nothing. Just the sound of his putting on clothing … yes, there was a zipper. A long one. I remember that. It sounded like the zipper sounds on a woman's housecoat."

"Have you had any salesmen at the door lately? Have you let anyone in the house—any strangers?"

"No. I'm gone most of the day. I work. I don't see many salesmen."

"Did he wear a mustache?" Martin demanded, still probing for clues.

"He was clean shaven. He smelled of after-shave lotion as if he had just shaved."

"Do you know what kind of lotion?"

"No, but I could identify it. It's different from the kind my husband uses."

"We'll check that out," the detective said, then added, "Have you noticed anyone watching you or following you?"

"No."

The detective consulted notes he had been making and closed the small notebook and put it in his pocket.

"If you can think of anything more … if you remember something … please get in touch with me."

Mary Jo nodded, then looked beyond him to the doorway as another man entered. She felt an unexplainable, burning blush creep over her face. Cal Horlick stood in the doorway exchanging a greeting with the detective.

"I've just finished questioning her," the detective explained. "We don't have much to go on." He quickly reviewed the information while the assistant district attorney listened intently.

"I'll check with you later," Horlick said when Martin finished. "We want this man."

"With any break, we'll get him," Martin said crisply and left the room. Horlick came toward the bed, a tall, lanky man with a thatch of rust colored hair and sharp blue eyes that now regarded Mary Jo with deep concern.

"Are you all right?" he demanded, a frown furrowing his brow.

"I'm all right, Cal," she said and managed to look at him.

"I couldn't believe it when I saw the report. Believe me, Mary Jo, we'll get him."

"I suppose that matters," she said softly, her tone bitter and reproachful. "Only to me it's—let's say, it's like locking the door after the horse is stolen."

Horlick placed his straw hat on a table and drew a chair to the side of the bed and sat down.

"That isn't what you want to say," he told her. "I know that you must feel dirtied, sullied, violated. There must be that, and you probably are bitter. You have a right to feel all that, and you're probably angry that I came here. But I had a reason."

"I suppose you did," she responded tartly.

"Let's put it this way, Mary Jo," Horlick said earnestly. "In one sense of the word you were violated—but in another you weren't even touched. All of us have bodies. Let's say that we just live in them. The important thing is what we, ourselves, are. He couldn't have touched you, even if he did molest your body."

"It's a nice thought, Cal. I wish I could believe it."

"You do, deep down. I just want you to know that others know it, too."

"How many others know about this, Cal? Is it all over town?"

"Very few. We're treating it as highly restricted information, and we'll keep your identity out of it. When we catch him, you'll have to appear, but we'll arrange that, too."

"Cal, I appreciate your coming here to see me. I know, too, that it's probably part of your job. But now I want to stop talking about it, or thinking about it—if I can. It's too ... intimate ... too personal."

He smiled sympathetically and got up from the chair. "I talked with the doctor and he says you can go home. He was going to call your husband. I'll leave you now."

She tried to return his smile, but she knew that her lips trembled and that she was on the verge of tears. She could find no reason for this, except that she didn't want to talk or to think about it for at least a few moments.

"Thank you, Cal," she murmured.

At the door he turned. "Listen, Mary Jo, if there's anything ... any time ... that I can do to help you, please let me know. Is that clear?"

"Yes, Cal."

"In a few days I'll probably have to talk with you again, and we'll be very objective about it. All right?"

"All right. Thanks, Cal."

He left and she closed her eyes. Before long a third man would come in to look at her and to think that she had been raped and taken by a man they didn't know. The third man would be the hardest to face. Her husband.

After a moment she opened her eyes and slowly got out of the bed. She found her clothes in a closet—the skirt and sweater she had somehow found and put on when she came from the bathroom. She had worn house slippers. She didn't remember putting them on. When she was dressed, she sat down in a chair to wait for Bill. She wondered what he would say to her, but most of all she wondered what she would say to him, and a small, disturbing twinge of uncertainty and nervousness took hold of her.

Bill arrived within a half hour, coming into the room slightly out of breath.

"Walked up," he explained. He looked searchingly into her face, his own expression strained and uneasy. "How are you, darling?"

She got up from the chair and went to him. "I'm all right, Bill." His arms went around her and she slid closely into his embrace. "The doctor says I can go home."

She looked up into his eyes and waited for his kiss. His lips touched hers for an instant, but it was not the kiss she had expected and wanted. She felt the slight withdrawal in him and there was nothing she could do or say about it. It was there, even if he did not realize it.

CHAPTER SEVEN
THELMA JORGSON

Monday morning Thelma Jorgson opened Dr. Mont's office promptly at nine o'clock. The doctor was making his morning calls and would not be in until after eleven, but there was plenty of work to do before patients began to arrive.

It was going to be another hot day, and she wore a white nylon uniform with very little beneath it. The office was not air-conditioned and by afternoon it would be stifling.

She opened the doctor's appointment book and quickly checked the day's patients. The last one was a Mrs. Miles and the name reminded her of Miles Salin and she again felt the angry chagrin she had experienced Saturday night.

How many hints did a man have to have? They could have gone to a show and at least taken a walk afterwards. Didn't he know that she lived next door to him? Slept within a few yards of him?

She smiled wryly as she thought about it, and her excuse about buying a used car so that she could talk with him and try to open the gate a little.

Yesterday she had considered the idea of a used car more seriously. A car could make a big difference to her, and possibly it could lead to a few dates with Miles Salin. Furthermore, she could afford the $500.

Anything would be better than going to shows alone on Saturday nights. Ever since she had broken with Dan she had discovered how hard it sometimes was for a girl to get another man. She might have been able to effect a reconciliation with Dan if he had not gone to Alaska on that construction job.

So now she went to movies alone on Saturday nights. And where had Miles Salin gone? She heard him come in sometime after midnight because she couldn't sleep and it was just midnight that last time she had looked at her clock. Sometime after that she heard him come in very quietly and move about in his room. A drawer had opened and closed with the same scraping noise she had heard on many occasions.

Later he had taken a shower and had returned to his room and moved about some more. If she could have dreamed up another excuse she would have knocked on his door. When she had insomnia she had a deep desire to share it with someone else. They could have talked, or perhaps …

"Well," she said to herself, "after all, it isn't as if Dan and I never did. You might as well be practical about it."

She put away the appointment book and made some entries in the bookkeeping system. The telephone rang and a patient cancelled an appointment. Thelma looked through the short list of names on a pad and selected one and told another patient that there was a cancellation and, "Doctor will see you at two this afternoon."

Dr. Mont had a small reputation as a gynecologist. At times Thelma wished that he had a general practice. At least, there would be male patients then. She had had a surcease of female patients and the multitude of disorders to which females were addicted.

"It would be nice to see a man walk in," she sometimes told Elizabeth, Dr. Halloway's nurse next door.

The idea about buying the used car came to her again and she decided that she would look into it more thoroughly. At least it would give her a chance to become better acquainted with the roomer next door, and Miles Salin had certainly volunteered to help her find a car. It might be smart to read up a little on photography, too. He had definitely shown interest when she had mentioned the darkroom in the basement.

Once again she wondered what had kept him out until after midnight on Saturday night. What would a man without a girl do on a Saturday night?

Cora Henshaw, the doctor's office nurse, came in. She looked red-eyed and tired.

"Specialing again?" Thelma asked.

"Mrs. Darwin. The registry didn't have a single special available on short notice, so Doctor asked me to take it just for one night. That old lady is a plain bitch, Thelma."

"A lot of them are."

"I probably look a wreck, and I've a date with Steve tonight."

"Sleep an hour. I'll call you."

"Fine. Make it two hours. Doctor won't mind. It got him off the spot last night. And you should see the house, Thelma. It's nice to have money like that."

"That's what Doctor thinks. You should see some of her bills."

Thelma watched the nurse go into a back examination room. She liked Cora and they got along well.

She thought about the car again and picked up the morning newspaper and looked through the classified section at used car ads. A Ford sedan priced at $500 caught her eye. She noted the dealer's name and read the description of the car again. At least, it was a place to start. The dealer's address was close to the parking lot where Miles Salin worked, and not far from her own office.

She glanced at her watch. Just 9:30. At noon she could stop by the parking lot and ask Miles. Maybe he'd take time to look at the car then, or he might stop by after work. Possibly they could have dinner together.

The car, she decided, was definitely a good idea. Already it was opening avenues of approach. And besides, she'd enjoy having a car.

She had a quick lunch in the downstairs drug store and hurried to the parking lot. Miles saw her and came out from the gas station enclosure where he was checking sales slips.

"I hate to bother you, Miles, but there's a car listed in the paper this morning," she explained. "It's down at the dealer's in the next block. I wonder if you'd have a chance to look at it today?"

She showed him the ad she had clipped from the newspaper.

"Might be all right," he decided. "I'm just going to lunch. Shall we walk down there and have a look?"

This was better than she had expected, and she fell into step beside him as they walked toward the used car lot.

"I didn't see you around the house yesterday," she said. "Were you out of town?"

"I left early and took some pictures. You gave me the idea the night before. Last night I asked Mrs. Lindicott. She said she'd be glad to let me use the darkroom, so I'm going to send for an enlarger and other stuff I left at my Uncle's."

"What kind of a camera do you have?"

He smiled, almost tolerantly. "Actually I have three, but the one I used mostly is an old Leica two with an F-two Summar lens."

She laughed a little. Her only experience with cameras had been the cheap box camera she had used in high school years before. "I'm afraid you're over my head already."

"It's a thirty-five millimeter camera. Takes small pictures for slides, or enlarging."

"I'd like to see some of your pictures sometime."

He looked at her with a friendly smile. "I like to do candid shots with a model. Maybe you could pose for me." He watched her closely, his expression quizzical and intent.

She wondered what he meant. Candid shots could mean anything. "How do you mean?" she asked.

"Oh, walking down the street, doing something with your hands, brushing your hair, reaching up on a shelf ... almost anything."

"I might model the new bathing suit I just bought," she smiled.

"Sure. You'd look good!"

"If I get the car maybe we can go swimming and you can take some pictures then."

"It's a long drive to the beach."

"Not over a couple of hours ... if you drive."

"Well, it's an idea. I haven't done anything interesting for a long time."

She risked another small laugh. "You must have found something interesting to do Saturday night. I heard you come in after midnight."

"Oh?" There was a sudden coolness in his voice and he glanced at her sharply. Then he smiled. "Well, it wasn't very exciting. It was so hot that I took a long walk up on the Heights until it cooled off."

They were nearing the used car lot and he began to stare at the cars lined up for inspection. "Looks like your car over there," he pointed.

A salesman came over as they stopped to inspect the car. He started his sales talk, but Miles cut him short.

"Look, drive it up to the garage in the next block with us and let a mechanic friend of mine have a look at it," he suggested.

The salesman nodded. "This is one time I will," he grinned. "This car is really clean, and that's the actual mileage on the speedometer. Good rubber, good engine, doesn't need any work. Our shop-man says there's even ten thousand miles of brake lining left. It's a good buy. Come on."

They got in the car and drove to the garage next to the parking lot. A gray haired man greeted Miles and met Thelma. "Let's run it on the lift and take a look underneath," he said, eyeing the car.

Within a few moments the mechanic substantiated the salesman's opinion of the car, but refused the five dollar bill she offered him. "You're a friend of Miles, and that's enough for me," he smiled.

"Well, Miss?" the salesman asked.

She looked at Miles and he nodded. "It's a good buy if you want it."

She had approximately $5,000 in the bank, and Dr. Mont paid her a good salary. It would take no great effort to buy the car.

"I'll take it," she decided. She hesitated a second. "I have to get back to the office by one and it's twenty to now. If you'll make out the papers—for a cash deal—and bring them to my office, I'll give you a check. Miles, would you mind driving it home for me this evening? I'll be nervous. It's been quite a while since I've driven."

Miles nodded. "Come around to the lot when you get through work and we'll pick it up."

With a small smile of satisfaction, Thelma thanked him. It began to look as if the rest of the summer was going to be all right; that she wouldn't go to so many shows alone; that perhaps the feelings Dan had awakened in her might not remain dormant now.

CHAPTER EIGHT
LIEUTENANT MARTIN

Shortly after 6 P.M. on Monday, Lieutenant Martin sat in a police car in front of Mrs. Lindicott's rooming house. So far the routine questioning in the neighborhod had failed to net him anything of value concerning the Saturday night attack upon Mary Jo Camman.

In the rooming house he had talked with Mrs. Lindicott, who had retired early Saturday night, and to two roomers. An elderly Mr. Crowth had also retired early, and a John Plinich had worked that night at the freight terminal where he was employed. Martin had checked out his story with a telephone call. Now two roomers were left, according to Mrs. Lindicott, and they should be home at any moment. Another one was out of town on vacation.

Ordinarily he would have had one of his men do the routine on this case, but Horlick seemed to be especially interested. It took time from what Martin considered to be more important problems, but Horlick was coming up fast in the city's political scene and a police lieutenant never hurt himself doing a good job for a man on the upbeat.

With any luck he could talk with the two remaining roomers and still be home in time for dinner.

From his car in front of the rooming house, his view of the Camman house was largely obscured by the towering old trees.

Only the bottom floor and the front entrance and the yard were visible from the street.

The day's heat still clung to the pavement and the interior of the car was hot, even with the windows and the right door open for ventilation. He wished the roomers would come home.

In the rear view mirror he saw a car turn into the street and coast to a stop behind him. A man and a woman got out.

He waited to see if they went into the rooming house, but they got out of the car and circled it, inspecting it carefully. He heard the man say, "You got a good buy, Thelma."

Martin got out of the police car and walked back to the parked car. The man and the woman looked at him questioningly. He introduced himself.

"I'm looking for Thelma Jorgson and Miles Salin," he explained.

"I'm Thelma Jorgson," the girl said nervously. "This is Mr. Salin. Is something wrong?"

"Just a few routine questions," Martin said. "I wonder if we could talk for a moment in my car." He looked at Salin and added, "I'd appreciate your waiting. It'll only take a few moments."

Thelma Jorgson accompanied him to his car and got in the front seat. He circled around to the other door and saw Salin go to the porch of the house and sit on a step.

"This won't take long, Miss Jorgson," he said. "There was an incident in the neighborhood late Saturday night. By any chance were you out? Did you see anyone—a man—around here who might have acted suspiciously?"

A puzzled frown was on her face as she thought back. "No ... no one who looked suspicious. I went to a movie and I don't recall seeing anyone in the block when I came home."

"Nothing at all? No car parked near here?"

"No. Maybe if I knew what it's all about ..."

"Just a police matter," Martin hedged.

"Miles—Mr. Salin may have seen someone. He got in after midnight. I'm sorry I can't help."

Martin thanked her and watched her walk to the house. Salin got up from the step and approached the car.

"Something wrong, Lieutenant?" he asked.

"A little trouble in the neighborhood Saturday night. Did you see a man anywhere in the vicinity late that night?"

Salin was thoughtful. "No, I don't recall seeing one. I went for a walk and got home after midnight. Too hot to sleep in my room early in the evening."

"You didn't see anyone else in this block when you came home?"

Salin was thoughtful again. "I vaguely recall someone walking away in the next block," he said. "Toward town."

"A man?"

"I'm not sure. I didn't pay much attention. I remember looking down the street and seeing someone. Seemed to be walking away in a hurry. What was it? Robbery?"

"Something like that. I may want to talk with you again. Where can I find you during the day?"

Miles Salin told him the location of the parking lot. "If I can help, let me know. But I'm afraid I can't. I just sort of remember someone walking away."

"That may help," Martin told him. "Thanks for your time."

Salin left the car and went into the rooming house. Martin decided that he'd have a man cover the next two or three blocks toward town in the morning. Someone may have seen the vague person Salin thought he had seen.

And if someone had seen a man hurry away, what about it? It was an inadequate description to help find one man in a city of half a million persons, Martin thought.

He started his car and headed toward home. He didn't like this case. There was virtually nothing with which to work. He could round up the known sex offenders in town and grill them, but it probably would avail him nothing. Most of them followed a set pattern—but none as elaborate or unique as this one had used. Nevertheless, he'd better pull in some of the worst ones in the morning.

They had discovered one thing during the day. Lab men had managed to trace the rope to a five and dime store. None of the clerks remembered a sale. But at least they knew that the purchase probably had been made in the city. If the store had been in the suburbs, it might have localized the area where the man lived, but the store was in the center of town. Anyone could have bought the rope there.

There had been no strange fingerprints, no footprints, nothing. Bruises on Mrs. Camman's arm indicated that the intruder's hands were fairly large. A vacuuming of the bed had brought forth no hairs, no foreign dust; nothing. Everywhere they had turned, the answer had been negative. And from the D.A.'s office came the persistent needling calls from Cal Horlick.

Martin spotted a telephone booth beside a filling station and stopped. Before he went home he'd better check with the office. Something might have come in. Sergeant McCloskey gave him a rundown on a few other developments in other cases.

"We're going to have trouble with the rapist," he concluded. "Do you think he'll repeat?"

"Probably. That's the pattern. Then we'll really be in trouble. Horlick will call out the Marines."

"Nothing in the neighborhood?"

"Nothing except an idea of one of the roomers at the corner place that he saw someone walk away shortly after midnight."

"How about the roomer?"

"I talked with his landlady. He checks out pretty well. Quiet and minds his own business. Works at a parking lot, and she thinks the girl in the room next to him has a case on him."

"So she's keeping an eye on them, huh?"

"Not particularly. Salin—that's his name—doesn't seem to be particularly interested in women."

"Sometimes those are the ones."

"I know. But what do I do? Haul him in because sometimes men who don't appear to be interested in women sometimes rape them?"

McCloskey laughed. "Okay. It was just an idea. You going home now?"

"Yeah. I'm almost late for dinner and Alice will give me hell if I don't get there or call. Something bothers me, though."

"Can't you tie it down?"

"No. Something I saw this afternoon. I can't get it. I don't even know what it is."

"Sometimes it works that way. You want me to call you at home if anything breaks, or are you going out?"

"I'll be watching TV."

"Mysteries?" McCloskey asked.

Martin grunted and hung up. He went back to the car and drove home slowly. It was true, he thought, he had seen something, or noticed something that bothered him. And he couldn't tab it.

What the sergeant had said bothered him, too. Once a man started a thing like this, it too often ran into a series. One more like this and the roof would be off!

"But I don't know how to stop it," he said aloud. "Damned if I do!"

CHAPTER NINE
MARY JO CAMMAN

On a Friday afternoon in September, Mary Jo got off a city bus and walked toward the old house. Bill had phoned that he would be a trifle late and couldn't pick her up after work. The bus had been crowded and she was tired. Hot weather had stayed on into September and the early evening was very warm. Only a few leaves had fallen and it still seemed like summer.

She turned the corner by Mrs. Lindicott's rooming house and gave a friendly smile to the couple getting out of a car in front of the place. They made a good-looking couple; the tall, blond young man and the blonde, well-proportioned woman. Evidently the girl recently had bought a car and she saw the couple together frequently. She supposed it was developing into one of those rooming house romances that would eventually end in marriage.

The thought of a romance and marriage brought a sick feeling to her. In a few weeks a cloud had grown rapidly and steadily over her own marriage; a cloud not of her making, but inspired by what had happened to her; an insidious, silent cloud that grew in intensity and brought with it the darkness and menace of impending disaster.

She had been acutely conscious of the strange withdrawal in Bill's kiss at the hospital the morning after, and the warmth she had once valued so much had failed to return.

That withdrawal had gone beyond the kisses in a strange evasion upon Bill's part that she knew worried him, yet an evasion that he seemed powerless to overcome.

The small warm intimacies that exist between a husband and wife were gradually disappearing or becoming mechanical and meaningless—the caress of a hand, the exchange of a glance, the small jokes and familiarities that a man and woman can share.

Not that Bill had not displayed concern and tenderness for her. He had. But not once since that night had there been more than that; no expression of his physical need for her. Her lips tightened a little as she walked and thought about it.

"To be blunt," she told herself, "he doesn't seem to want me sexually."

She got out her key and let herself into the house and went to the bedroom to change into a housedress. The trend of her thoughts had awakened her sensitivity to the room and subconsciously her eyes avoided the bed.

She had disposed of the spread that had covered it that night and she thought of converting one of the two spare bedrooms into a master bedroom, but the rooms were smaller and she told herself that the best way to overcome the memory was to face it and live with it until it no longer mattered. If that time could ever come.

She decided upon a shower before she put on the housedress, and disrobed and went to the bathroom. The water felt refreshing and she was drying herself with a big bath towel when she heard Bill call to her from downstairs. She opened the bathroom door and replied to him, and heard him come up the stairs. She slipped into a terry cloth robe and entered the bedroom where he was hanging his coat in a closet.

"Got through earlier than I expected," he explained. "I tried to get you at the office before you left, but I missed you."

She went to her bed and lay down to relax for a few moments. "Rough day?" she asked conversationally.

"Pete and Art are down with the flu. Rough enough." He stripped to his shorts and took a pair of blues from his closet and got into them before he moved to his own bed to sit down and look at her wearily.

"You look bushed, too," he said.

"Not really. It was hot at the office," she said. She stretched a little, knowing that her robe had parted and that his gaze was upon her. She shut her eyes and rested her arms back over her head.

After a moment he moved and she felt his weight on the bed as he sat beside her and his fingers idly opened the terry robe farther.

"You're a beautiful woman," he said softly. "Really beautiful."

She smiled without opening her eyes and said, "I'm glad you think so, Bill. Lately I've wondered."

He leaned over and kissed her. A hand gently sought her breast. "I've never thought otherwise," he said.

"You haven't loved me lately," she chided him, her voice husky.

"I've never stopped loving you from the moment I first saw you."

"That isn't what I mean ..." She stirred slightly in a subtle movement of receptiveness. His lips pressed against her mouth again with greater force and his hand tightened a trifle.

"It's all right if you want to ..." she murmured.

She felt him get up from the bed and heard the sound of clothing being removed and, still with her eyes closed, she squirmed out of the robe.

He returned to her and his lips were on hers again and she felt the familiarity of his hands caressing her. She smiled and her hands found him and urged him on.

But the moment was strangely delayed beyond expectation and she detected a frantic determination in his kisses. Sensing his frustration, she tried to help him, beginning to feel the sharpness of her own need and the torture of waiting. Abruptly he pushed away from her and his voice was troubled.

"I can't, Mary Jo ... it's no use. I want to ... but I can't."

She opened her eyes and looked up. His face was flushed and troubled and there was a harried expression in his glance. It was as if he were asking for help that she was unable to give.

"You're tired," she said, knowing that this was not the answer to what was plaguing him.

He shook his head. "It's not that."

So it *was* the other, she thought. Perhaps in saying it, there would be a washing away of it.

"It's because of what happened," she said quietly. "Don't be ashamed to say it, Bill. I can understand."

"I guess so," he admitted in a defeated voice.

"Maybe it will help if we talk it out. Why don't you ask me questions? If there are things you want to know, I'll tell you."

He stared at her, a light blush coming to his cheeks. "You wouldn't mind?"

"No."

"I guess it bothers me. I try to be rational about it, and sensible. You couldn't help what happened, but maybe if I knew, the other would leave me."

"I know. You're a man and you're possessive. But I can't tell you unless you ask me. I don't know where to start, or what you really want to know. Is it the details? Is that what you have to know?"

"I think so. I'm not sure."

"You want to know exactly what he did? Because I'm your wife and I belong to you ... is that it?"

"I think so."

"If he hurt me? Things like that?"

"Yes."

"I thought he was going to hurt me, but he didn't. Not really. It was as if I were standing by and watching two other persons. That the things weren't happening to me."

"What things, Mary Jo?"

Suddenly she wished that she had not suggested this pseudo-psychiatric purging. There was something unhealthy and sordid about it. There was too much of a strange, tense, anguished excitement creeping into Bill's voice.

She shut her eyes again and carefully chose her words.

"Do you remember the books about sex and marriage we read when we were first married, Bill? It was like that."

"How do you mean?"

"The things he did. It was almost as if he had memorized the instructions about love play and was intent upon following them to the letter."

"Did he do things that I don't do ... we don't do?"

She hesitated, and knew then that he would persist in his mental probing until he was satisfied. Perhaps it was better to tell him. Then, maybe, it could end once and for all.

"Yes ... a few things."

"With his hands?"

"Yes."

"Did he hurry?"

"No, he didn't hurry. Bill, are you sure you want to hear these things? It doesn't matter now. I told you. I wasn't there. It was happening to someone else."

"But you could feel it."

"Yes. How could I help it?"

"He used his mouth ... ?"

"Yes."

"What did it do to you, Mary Jo?"

"Stop it, Bill! We can't talk this way. It's … it's …"

"And then he took you," he said tensely. "For a long time, Mary Jo? I've got to know. Tell met!"

"I … I don't know, Bill. Please!"

"Did you, Mary Jo? *Did you?*"

A cold fear came over her now because there was a new note of intensity in his voice, and he was asking the question she must not answer.

"Please, Bill …"

Abruptly he had drawn back from her. When she opened her eyes he was looking at her with an expression she could not interpret.

"You did," he said softly. "You had an orgasm."

"Bill! I'm your wife! Can't you understand … ?" Hot tears welled up in her eyes. Didn't he understand? It had not been of her making. It had not been a betrayal. Yet his voice carried the unreasonable overtones of accusation, and she had *lied*.

She tried to sit up, but his hands came to her shoulders and forced her back. He was breathing quickly now and his mouth was set and hard.

"You're mine," he said fiercely. "Remember that."

Then he was taking her with the same ferocity that his voice had betrayed—roughly, unheedingly, and without words or affection. After a moment she lay passive, tears slowly running down her cheeks, and in the onslaught upon her she could think only one thing: *This is rape.*

When he was finished he left her abruptly and went to the bathroom. After a moment, Mary Jo rose and put on the terry robe and went to her dressing table. She sat there, gazing at her own reflection until he returned and dressed and stood behind her, their eyes meeting in the mirror.

"I'm sorry," he said, the corners of his mouth drooping. "I don't know what came over me. I don't understand it."

"Perhaps you had to let me know that I'm yours."

"I didn't have to be primitive." He was uncertain and his eyes were troubled. "I hope I didn't hurt you."

"No." She stood up and faced him. He took her in his arms with a gentleness that had been absent in his lovemaking. "Just hold me a moment," she said.

"You didn't get much out of that," he said flatly.

She realized that it was a half question and that he was hoping for denial. A man's vanity never deserted him. She knew better than to disparage him. "Yes, I did, Bill. It was different. For this once. I did, and I know who my man is."

"I think things will be all right now, Mary Jo. And once again—I'm sorry."

"You needn't be, darling. Let's forget it now. Meanwhile, let's eat! I'm starved. You go down and put on the coffee."

He smiled and apparently he had found what he wanted in the conversation. He kissed her again lightly and went down stairs.

"He's a man," she thought. "And it isn't finished. Only for the moment. Maybe it will never be finished."

A month had passed since the night when she had been violently awakened and forced into an act that had created this change in her husband, and, perhaps, in herself. For three weeks there had been the heavy fear that she might be pregnant, but she had escaped that.

She had hoped that, with the passing of that fear, she and Bill might enter into a new cycle of understanding and adjustment that would magically set things right. Now she knew that if there was a new cycle in their marriage, it was not to be a return to their previous easy relationship.

Thoughtfully she dressed and went downstairs to the kitchen. Bill had put on a percolator of coffee and was setting the table.

"I'd settle for ham and eggs," he said. "I thought we might hurry it and go to a show."

"Carrie called me at the office. She thought we might go over there. We haven't seen much of them lately."

"Good idea."

Mary Jo went to the refrigerator and got out eggs and ham, remembering the telephone call from Carrie. There had been an odd note of concern in Carrie's voice, and suddenly Mary Jo realized that they had not spent an evening with the couple for over a month.

"Bill, do they know?" she asked abruptly. She turned with the food and looked at him where he was pouring a first cup of coffee at the stove. He didn't look at her, but nodded.

"They know."

"Did you tell them?" A slight edge was in her voice.

He tasted the coffee and looked at her over the top of the cup. "I didn't tell them, Mary Jo. Remember that Al is a newspaperman. He knew about it the Monday after it happened and spoke to me about it. I asked him not to say anything to Carrie, but I suppose he finally did."

"I don't know why I'm annoyed," she admitted. "Carrie has been my best friend for years."

"Maybe they think it's strange that we haven't seen them," Bill said.

"No. They've been busy every weekend. Something to do with church dinners. They're trying to raise money to do some repairs on the church."

"What will you do if Carrie asks you about it?"

"I don't know. I suppose I'll tell her. It's just that I don't want to talk about it." She broke eggs into a skillet. "Do you want to go over there?"

"Let's. Maybe it will be good for us. I'll call them."

They had just finished the dishes when the doorbell rang. Bill answered it and Mary Jo heard men's voices. In a few moments Bill called to her.

She hurried into the front room and found Lieutenant Martin standing there. The sight of him stirred a nervous apprehension in her. She acknowledged his greeting with a hesitant smile and asked him to sit down. She sat across the room from the couch where Bill had seated himself with the detective.

Bill said, "Lieutenant Martin has some news."

Martin shook his head. "Not specific news, Mrs. Camman, but something has happened that may give us a lead."

She waited, not knowing what to say, and disturbed by the Lieutenant's seriousness.

"You were blindfolded that night," he said. "Were there enough folds of that bandage so that you couldn't tell if the light in the room was on or off?"

"Could I see light through the bandages? No. I knew that he turned on the bedlamp because I heard the click. But I couldn't detect any light."

The detective nodded. "Do you remember hearing any clicks when he was away from you?"

"No. Why?"

"We're wondering if he took any pictures before he left."

"Pictures!" She felt a quick blush of embarrassment and shook her head uncertainly. "I don't know. You mean the flash from a flashbulb? I couldn't have known. And I didn't hear any click. I hope not. What makes you think he might have?"

"Within the last ten days there have been two attacks on other women—at least two that have been reported to us."

"You mean like the attack on me?"

"Not quite. In both cases we know about, it happened to couples parked out on country roads. A man wearing a hood over his head suddenly appeared at a car door with a gun. He forced the couple to leave the car and walk into woods with him where he made the girl tie her escort's hands behind his back with his arms around the trunk of a tree, and then gag him with tape. Afterwards he took the girl farther into the woods. He forced her to undress and then tied her hands and gagged her. He took several flash pictures of her before and after he attacked her, then left her. Each girl managed to find her escort and untie him."

"You think it's the same man?"

"Our lab men are certain that the rope comes from the same length used by the man who attacked you. And the same tape used as a gag. You didn't get a glimpse of him? You're sure?"

"No."

"Please think back carefully. Was there any time when he might have taken pictures of you?"

"No. I'm quite certain. There wasn't time after he tied me, and I heard him leave immediately after he dressed. I could identify those sounds, and I'm certain I heard no camera clicks, nor the sound of bulbs being changed in a flash gun."

Martin stood. "We're reasonably sure it's the same man. He's added the picture taking to his routine. I don't want to alarm you, but I think it would be better if you keep the house securely locked if you're alone evenings, Mrs. Camman."

"Then there's danger?"

"Who knows exactly how a distorted mind works?" asked the lieutenant. "If he gets a perverted pleasure in taking the pictures and looking at them afterwards, it can become a powerful obsession with him. If he didn't get pictures of you—under the more ideal circumstances of the attack upon you—he may develop a compulsion to get those pictures. He may come back."

Bill Camman stared at the detective. "For God's sake, Martin, can't you get him? Do we have to live in constant fear that he'll come back? Can't you do something to—"

"We're doing everything we can," Martin interrupted quietly. "I'm as concerned as you are, and I don't want to alarm you unnecessarily. But we can't afford to fake chances. Do you work nights often, Camman?"

"About every third Saturday night."

"When you're on night shift let us know. We'll have a car drive by occasionally," Martin said. He turned to Mary Jo. "On those nights leave plenty of lights on in the house and keep your blinds pulled. You'd better leave the porch light on, too."

He moved toward the door and hesitated. "Please don't worry too much about this. With any luck we'll have him within a few days."

Bill said, "Perhaps I should get a gun."

The detective shook his head. "I wouldn't advise it. If anything should happen and he faced a gun he might be much more dangerous. We don't want murder."

Bill went to the door with him and Mary Jo sat quietly in the living room thinking about the detective's words. She was certain that no pictures had been taken, but she could sense that the man might want to return for pictures. She shuddered.

CHAPTER TEN
MILES SALIN

Thelma Jorgson knocked on his door three nights after she had bought the car, and when he opened it she offered him two keys. Miles took them automatically and then stood holding them with a puzzled frown and a question in his eyes.

"What are these?"

"A key to the car and one to the garage I just rented. It's around the corner. One of those four single garages by the old frame house. It only costs me five dollars a month."

"But I don't want to—" he started to protest. She interrupted him in a decisive tone of voice.

"Now please don't object, Miles. I'll feel better if someone else has the keys to the car. Besides, I want you to use it as much as you like."

For a moment he was on the verge of handing the keys back to her with a flat refusal, but he suddenly realized that she was making a car available to him. Furthermore, the garage was half a block away and out of sight of the house. Now late at night instead of taking a walk, he could take a ride and no one would ever know; not even Thelma.

He also realized that she was trying to cement the relationship between them. Well, he could handle that, and there was no use in turning down the offer of a car.

He still appeared to be a little reluctant, but he nodded and said, "I'll keep them for you in case of an emergency. If you're sure you want me to have them. I won't use the car, though. I don't want to do that."

"Use it as much as you like, Miles. It's insured and I really won't drive it much."

"Well, maybe once in a while. But it's understood that I pay for the gas and oil I use."

"It's a deal then!" She seemed happy to get his acceptance of the keys. "I was wondering, too, about parking on your lot."

"I can fix that."

"Then you can ride to work with me in the mornings and come home with me."

He avoided tying himself down definitely. "Sometimes I stay overtime. But I guess we could ride to work together every morning."

She looked beyond him into his room, as if seeking an invitation to come in, and noticed his camera on a table. "Oh, is that the Leica you told me about?"

Why not? he thought. "Come in and take a look at it," he invited. He opened the door wider and she came in at once, crossing to the table to examine the camera. "Is this the one that takes the small pictures for slides?" she asked.

"I enlarge a lot of them, too," he said, closing the door. He looked at her back, the outline of her buttocks, the firm, tapering legs, and suddenly he could imagine her in the nude, and a strong surge of desire for her swept through him. He fought it. This was one woman he would have to leave alone, or play carefully. He walked over behind her and reached around, picked up the camera, and made a pretense of showing it to her.

"Don't you have some pictures you've taken with it?" she asked.

She looked up into his face and he sensed, at once, that she wasn't really interested in pictures. Well, if she was interested in other things, maybe he could shock her a little or embarrass her.

"I've a few enlargements," he admitted. He went to a dresser drawer and brought out an envelope thick with pictures and selected one for her to look at.

She took it with a feigned show of interest and then glanced at it and her expression changed and a slight blush crept to the roots of her hair.

"Oh! She's ... really lovely."

"Beautiful," he said solemnly taking the enlargement from her and looking at the picture of the nude girl. The girl had not known that he had taken the picture. It was one of the best shots he had ever obtained. It was just luck that he had been on that isolated part of the beach asleep when he heard movement not far from him and the large driftwood log behind which he had spread a blanket.

Cautiously he had looked over the top of the log and the girl was undressing, obviously a victim of impulse, and unaware that anyone was within miles of the small inlet.

When she was undressed she had run down to the surf and plunged in for a few moments and then raced back, not glancing at the tangled mass of driftwood where he had concealed himself. He had shot the picture quickly, and several more before she had dressed.

There was no point in telling Thelma the circumstances, however. She could think what she liked. And now she smiled a little like a conspirator.

"Was she one of your girlfriends?" she asked.

Miles shrugged indifferently and saw a new look of respect come into her eyes. He enjoyed seeing the look, and he wondered if the picture, and the idea she must have, excited her.

"It doesn't mean anything," he said. "No more than to an artist painting a nude. Photography is an art, too. The female nude is one of the finest art studies."

"I suppose so," she said seriously. "But didn't you have trouble getting her to pose?"

"Would it bother you?"

"I'm afraid I wouldn't be much of a study," she laughed in embarrassment.

"But you would," he told her. "You'd make a fine study."

"Well, don't ask me!"

He didn't press the point and put the picture away. "Lately I've been concentrating on studies of the city. I've written for my enlarger and by next week I should be at work in the darkroom."

She had walked away from the table and sat in the chair she had occupied on her previous visit.

"You're an odd man, Miles," she said.

"Odd? How?" He went over to his bed and sat on it.

"You seem to live within yourself. You never go out with girls. Yet you find enjoyment in doing really good photography of nudes. I'll bet you're very creative."

"Maybe. I don't know."

"What are you going to do with your life? You must want something?" She spoke now with the same gentle prodding that she had heard Doctor use on patients.

He shrugged. "I'm not sure yet. I'm not thirty. There's plenty of time."

"It just seems that working in a parking lot isn't like you," she said. "Not that it isn't good work, but ..."

"It's just a stop-gap job."

"Then you do have something planned for the future?"

"The right thing will come along." He didn't like her questions. He didn't know what he wanted to do with the rest of his life. How could he, when it was all such a confusion right now? Earning a living was a bore. A means to an end. The main thing was to satisfy the queer desires of his body. They must be different from the desires other men had. Or were they?

Sometimes when he took his walks late at night he looked at the houses, the apartment buildings, the hotels, and wondered about the men and women who were bedded down in them. He tried to imagine how it would be to sleep nights with a woman, and he tried to be certain within his own mind of the relationship that exists between a married couple.

To have a woman ready to serve you with her body whenever you desired. To have breasts to be bared to you, the familiarity of panties and bra for you to take off the body of a woman, the freedom to caress and take in the security of your own room with no chance for interruption; no law to be broken.

And at these times he was occasionally tempted with the thought of taking a wife, but immediately the thought of supporting her and taking on the added responsibility, bringing an end to his independence, was too great to overcome.

And in Thelma he saw a trap. But it did not need to be a trap, he thought. If he were careful, he could control this. He could experiment—use persuasion and cunning to get what he wanted from her. He could always leave when he tired of her. He could move to another city. No one could hold him here against his wishes.

He could start now, though, with a new experiment, and the idea set up a sudden tumult of emotion within him.

"Would you pose for me?" he asked abruptly.

Her eyes widened a trifle and she looked at him with a startled expression. "You mean in the nude? I should say not! I—"

He forced a quick smile. "No, of course, not! But you mentioned a new bathing suit and that you'd pose in it. I thought you meant it and I'd like to try some lighting effects."

"You mean here?"

"Why not? Right now. I've some flood lights and reflectors. You can go in and change and we can take a roll or two. Then I'll have something to work with when my enlarger comes."

She considered the idea for a moment, then nodded. "It would be sort of fun, wouldn't it!"

"Of course!"

"I'd make a terrible model. But if you just want to try some lighting effects, that would be different."

He smiled inwardly as he listened to her convince herself that she should do it.

"If you weren't planning to go out this evening ..."

"No, I hadn't planned anything."

"Then you'll do it?"

"All right. Just this once so you can experiment with your lighting. Do you really want me to put on the bathing suit? Wouldn't this dress do just as well?"

"It would help a lot because I want to see how I come out with skin tones with some new film I have. They're hard to get just right."

"All right. I'll go and change."

With a mounting sense of excitement Miles got out flood lights and cheap, clamp-on reflectors. He took the spread from his bed and rigged a backdrop and put a blanket on the floor. They would serve as props.

Thelma came in without knocking and she wore the bathing suit. He hadn't realized how well formed she was. Firm, pointed breasts thrust against the cloth of the bathing suit and there was a mature, inviting swell to her hips and a lush fullness to her thighs that made it difficult for him to keep his eyes on her face after the first encompassing glance.

"You look like a million!" he said. "Just right for these shots. I fixed a blanket and backdrop and lights for the shots."

Self-consciously she walked to the blanket, then stared at him helplessly. "What do you want me to do?"

"First, let's take a shot looking down. Stretch out on your back and just look up, maybe with your arms thrown back easily."

As he placed the lights and attached the camera to a tripod she struck a pose more easily than he had expected. He focused the camera, bent over and moved one of her arms a trifle, and started to snap a short series of pictures. After the first few she was more at ease.

"You're a natural model," he told her. "I'll bet you could make money at it."

"I'm not that good," she protested, obviously pleased.

He turned off the flood lights and unscrewed the camera from the tripod. "That's enough for tonight. Let's see how these Come out and we can try some others later on."

She sat on the blanket watching him. "Do you think these will be any good?"

"They should be."

He sat on the blanket beside her and offered her a cigarette. They smoked in silence for a moment. He reached for an ashtray from the table and put it in front of them. After smoking her cigarette halfway down, she slowly put it out and lay back on the blanket, stretching so that the thrust of her breasts was obvious and inviting.

"This has been fun," she said.

He put out his cigarette, conscious of her breasts and the enticing whiteness of her thighs. Maybe he could carry the experiment just a little further—this new game that he had never deliberately tried before.

He leaned over her and bent down slowly. She shut her eyes and he kissed her, feeling her arms slide about his neck, pulling him down to her, and feeling the hotness of her breath against his mouth.

Moments later she whispered, "Wait!" She squirmed away from him and got up and went to the switch by the door and snapped out the lights. He saw her in the dim light as she took off the bathing suit, and he stood and quickly undressed. They came together on the bed in a hard, relentless union.

Her violence almost frightened him for now he was not in command, and she was not doing his bidding. She was demanding and enveloping and certain. He had the instinctive feeling that he was being used. He was not the aggressor, not the master but the victim.

It was over suddenly and completely and the only sounds were those of exhaustion and the tired, final cringing of bed springs as they moved away from each other.

He didn't know what to say, nor what to do. This was beyond his experience. He was almost startled when he heard her laugh softly.

"And I objected to posing in the nude!" she mused. She rose from the bed and picked up her bathing suit. "I'd like to stay," she said, "but I'd better not tonight. I'll see you in the morning."

"You can stay," he said then, thinking that there was more to be had from the night.

"We'll try it again soon," she said. "Good night, Miles. Did anyone ever tell you that you're good? Really good?" She laughed again very quietly, then she was gone.

Miles sat up on the side of the bed and smiled to himself. It hadn't been as good as the woman across the street, but it had been all right. Very much all right.

As for pictures of nudes, he had a plan for that, too. It had occurred to him at work the day before and he'd spent the afternoon on the job carefully working out details.

He'd get pictures of nudes for his collection; better than some of those Jap pictures. And he'd have some girls and women, too. He'd handle them like he had the woman across the street. Maybe he'd even go back there and see her again. She'd liked it that first time. She had tried not to, but she did. Better in some ways than Thelma. And the next time he'd take pictures. Maybe he could rig it so that he appeared in some of the photos.

He could do that with Thelma, too, with infra red. She'd never know. After a while he wouldn't need the Jap pictures. He'd have his own.

But he needed a gun. His plan for the other girls wouldn't work without a gun. And he knew where to get it. Lately he'd been closing the lot at six o'clock. There was a gun in the drawer under the cash register. He could take it for the night and no one would ever know.

He heard Thelma walk down the hallway to the bathroom and he smiled in the darkness of the room, then went to his window and looked across at the old house. The bedroom window was dark.

He put on an old robe and switched on the television set, putting on the earphones so that Thelma wouldn't know he still was awake.

The next morning Thelma tapped on his door as he was about ready to leave. He opened it and she came in and kissed him lightly before he could say "Good morning." There was a slight attitude of ownership in the way the kiss was delivered and in her bland smile.

"I slept wonderfully," she said. "Are you about ready? I thought maybe we could breakfast together."

Well, it was starting now. He wished for a second that he had never invited her into the room, and that he had maintained the barrier between them. But there was the car to consider and all the rest of the things he had thought about. If he took her and the rest of it for what it was worth, he wouldn't be hurt.

"Okay," he nodded. "Let's go."

They left the house and walked around the corner to the garage. He used the garage key she had given him to unlock the door and backed the car out while she waited. They drove down town while she kept up a chatter of small talk. He parked at a small cafe near the lot and they ate breakfast quickly while she discussed some of the patients that came to the doctor's office.

"You mean you have nothing but women patients?" he asked.

"Doctor is a gynecologist. Nothing but women—until I'm sick and tired of them."

"Then you probably know quite a bit about women."

She smiled slyly. "Quite a bit. Enough so that you don't have to worry about last night."

"Worry?"

"I won't get pregnant. Don't most men worry about that?"

He hadn't thought much about it. Suddenly he wondered if he had done that to the woman across the street. She'd have plenty to remember him for if he had!

This made a difference, though, about his feeling concerning Thelma. If he didn't have to worry about that, he could enjoy their relationship more. She would have no hold over him.

"Yeah," he said thoughtfully. "I suppose you know all about that. Working for that doctor."

"I do."

He finished his coffee and glanced at the clock. "I have to work until six for a few weeks. Maybe you'd better go home without me. I'll park the car for you on the lot, though."

"I won't mind waiting. We can eat together."

"If it won't make it too late for you. Maybe my enlarger will come today. I thought I'd develop and print the pictures we took if it did."

"Will you show me how to develop and print? I'd like to learn."

If she got interested in photography maybe she wouldn't be so reluctant to do some posing in the nude, he thought.

"I'll teach you."

She insisted upon paying her own check and he drove her to her office building and then parked the car in the lot.

During the day he further explored his plans to use her car at nights and he checked to make certain that the gun was in the drawer under the cash register.

They ate together that evening and when they arrived at the rooming house he learned that his enlarger had been delivered. His uncle had carefully packed it and sent it with other equipment by motor freight. Miles immediately set it up in the darkroom and Thelma came down to watch him work with the first pictures they had taken.

"They flatter me," she said when she saw the enlarged prints.

"You'd be a wonderful study in the nude."

"You should know!" she giggled. "But I won't pose that way. What if some of the pictures got out?"

"How could they? They'd be ours."

"No. I'm too bashful. Do you want to make love tonight?"

He laughed a little at her incongruity and shook his head. "Not tonight. I'm too tired. We had a rough day at the lot."

"We have plenty of time," she said softly and turned to him and pressed against him. "Haven't we?"

He kissed her, knowing that she expected it and enjoying the feel of her body against him. For a moment he was tempted, but he had made other plans for the night and it was almost ten o'clock now.

"Maybe tomorrow night," he said.

"I'll be ready, darling."

He recoiled a little at the word. Again there was the insinuation of ownership, but he supposed he'd have to get used to talk like this. It was small enough price to pay for what he was gaining!

"Let's get a good sleep tonight," he said. "Ready to go up?"

After she helped him put away the equipment they went upstairs to their rooms. In the kitchen Mrs. Lindicott was listening to her radio.

Miles waited until he was certain that Thelma was asleep, then dressed in his coveralls and jacket. He gathered together his pieces of rope, his hood, the tape. He took the gun from the inside pocket of the jacket he had worn from work. He checked it, making certain that it was loaded, and experimenting with the safety catch. Satisfied that he could use it without trouble, he put it in a side pocket of the jacket he intended to wear. Finally he checked the Leica and flash equipment, wrapping them in a cheap cotton car robe.

The hallway was quiet and Mrs. Lindicott's radio had been silenced. She slept in a back room near the kitchen on the first floor. He could leave safely by the front door and he had a key to let him in when he returned.

He walked around the corner to the garage, opened the door with extreme care and backed the car out, closing the door afterwards. He drove down a side street, then turned into a main highway climbing up into the Heights and the Highway and side roads beyond that led into wooded areas.

It was a half hour before he spotted a car parked on a lonely side road. He drove past it slowly and saw the couple embracing in the car. A quarter of a mile farther on he pulled off the road and parked behind underbrush.

He walked back in the darkness toward the parked car, and when he was within sight of it he stopped to put on the black hood and get out the gun. He checked the lengths of rope he had brought and the adhesive tape. He carried the blanket-wrapped camera in his left hand, the gun in his right.

Carefully he approached the car. The couple was in the back seat and the girl's sweater was rolled high. The man—he looked hardly more than a boy—was caressing the girl and pleading with her in a low voice. The girl's eyes were shut and she was shaking her head back and forth.

They didn't know that Miles was there until he opened the door and pressed the gun against the back of the man's head.

It was two o'clock when he wearily returned to his room. The house was quiet and he silently put away his equipment and undressed.

The girl had sobbed and there had been a cry of pain, muffled by the tape over her mouth, when he had finally possessed her. There had been blood, too. He smiled in the darkness of his room as he lay in bed with open eyes and remembered. She'd remember, too. All the rest of her life. And in the Leica were pictures of her.

Idly he wondered if the couple would report the attack to the police. Maybe they wouldn't. This was different from the couple across the street. And it made little difference if they did. Who could ever identify him?

He went to sleep making plans for the future. He could find plenty of parked cars on the country roads in back of the Heights. He could find plenty of girls, take pictures, and maybe the restless hunger … the dark, dark hunger in him would finally be appeased.

CHAPTER ELEVEN
LIEUTENANT MARTIN

After Martin talked with the Cammans he returned to head-quarters although he had long since put in a full day's work and was tired enough to go home.

On his desk he found a note to the effect that Chief Tom Ansel wanted to see him as soon as he returned to headquarters that night.

For a moment Martin was tempted to ignore the command, but thought better of it. He had to talk with Ansel sooner or later about the subject he knew was of greatest importance at the moment. There was no point in postponing it.

Sitting across a desk from the chief, he noticed the worry lines in the man's weather-seamed face. The chief was getting old. The job was beginning to tell on him, but he still maintained his habit of long hours on the job and his penchant for keeping track of everything that went on in the department.

Like every officer on the force, Martin never knew exactly where he stood with the older man. Deserved praise had been forthcoming from Ansel, and just criticism had been poignant and to the point.

Now Ansel looked at his subordinate with his pale blue eyes that could be completely devoid of expression, and his lips were set grimly.

"What are you doing about these attacks on women? The parked car cases?" he asked.

"Everything we can," Martin said. He gave a quick rundown and explained the rope and tape clues.

"Horlick is riding us," Ansel said. "He hasn't let up since the rape-attack on the Camman woman. He suggested this morning that I might be smart to take you off the case."

Martin carefully concealed a quick rise of anger. "Sorry he feels that way about it," he said. "I'm doing my best."

"Maybe that's not enough, Martin."

"That's up to you, sir."

"All right. Don't get touchy. I know you're doing everything you can. I told Horlick as much. He seems to have a special interest in the Camman case. Any idea why?"

"He mentioned something about their being old friends. The husband works for a wire service."

"I know that. The papers are getting on me, too."

"I'm sorry we haven't turned up more."

Ansel shook his head and lit a cigarette, the white cylinder looking oddly small for his large hand and heavy face. "The lab is certain about the rope?" he asked.

"We got a break there. Only one store handles that particular brand. We've alerted clerks. The guy leaves the ropes at the scene of attack and he'll eventually use up his supply."

"He could buy rope at a dozen other places, or more. It's ordinary clothesline. Any brand would do."

Martin nodded.

The chief thoughtfully contemplated his cigarette. "You checked out the neighborhood where the Cammans live?"

"I did most of it myself."

"Checked out the known perverts in town?"

"Yes."

"Any ideas about this man?"

"A few. He's probably a psycho, but there hasn't been any special indication of the sadist. At least, from what I know about it. From the Camman woman's story, he even may figure himself to be a Don Juan. Took lots of time with her, and some unusual techniques for a rapist."

"What about the others?"

"He worked faster with them. Took a lot of pictures. Some deliberately pornographic. The girls don't like to talk about it. And, of course, he wore the hood. That would hamper the Don Juan techniques."

"Do you think there have been any other cases besides the two reported?"

"You know how it is. Some people won't report them. Too ashamed or too frightened. And sometimes a wife is out with the wrong man when something like this happens, or a husband out with the wrong woman."

Ansel sighed. "Makes it tougher for us. Have you asked the county to keep a close watch on those back roads?"

"Yes. The newspapers—as you know—have run a couple of stories, too. That may scare off a few neckers from parking out there."

"Did he take pictures of the Camman woman?"

"No. I just stopped by and asked them to be careful. If the guy is on this kick he may come back. You never know what a son-of-a-bitch like that is going to do."

"All right. I guess you're doing everything you can. Remember, though, that Horlick is riding you. I'll protect you as much as I can. But, for Christ's sake, try to clean it up. We're going to be in trouble if it isn't stopped, or if that bastard kills someone."

"I know that." Martin got up and looked down at the chief. "If one of the boyfriends puts up a scrap, we may have worse than rape on our hands."

"We'll have the whole damned city on our necks. And maybe we should. Get on it, Martin. I'm leaving you in charge."

Martin went to his office. He checked reports. So far the night had been quiet. Maybe he could get a good sleep and some rest if he went home now.

Only now there was something else to worry about. If Cal Horlick was riding him, it could become rough before it got better.

The assistant D.A. was out to make a name for himself, and he wasn't above using some criticism in his news releases to strengthen his cause. A few biting remarks about the "inefficiency" of the police department and Lieutenant George Martin wouldn't make life any more secure at the Martin household.

He left headquarters and drove home slowly, lost in thought, trying to hit upon some one thing he might have overlooked in his investigation.

Alice was watching television when he arrived home. She greeted him with a smile.

"Did you have a good dinner downtown?" she asked.

Martin nodded wearily and sat down in an easy chair and glanced at the TV screen. He watched a quiz contestant answer a question correctly and lit a cigarette.

"Trouble?" Alice asked.

"The rapist," he said. "Horlick is on it now. I've just had a talk with Ansel."

"You're doing everything you can," she said with conviction.

"Ansel knows it. Horlick probably does, too. But a little more of this and the newspapers are going to get into the act. Then the public really puts on the pressure. And I'm at the bottom getting all of it."

She was silent, watching the screen and not paying attention to it.

"George, what makes a man do things like that?"

"If I were a psychiatrist maybe I could tell you, Alice. I simply don't know. All I know is that there are men like that running around loose."

"I wonder how a woman feels after she's been taken by force by a stranger," she mused.

"Soiled, I imagine. Would you?"

"Yes."

"There's another angle that's troublesome," he stated. "Even though it isn't the wife's fault, some husbands seem to blame the wife. I suppose it's a form of jealousy—knowing that another man has had his wife."

"Would you feel that way about me?"

He grinned at her. "With a couple of football players around to look after you, I don't worry about it."

"No. Seriously. How do you think you'd feel?"

He looked at her tenderly. "First, I'd want to let you know that everything was all right between us. And then I'd go looking for the man. Let's not talk about it. I'd rather watch TV."

At precisely three o'clock the next morning, a few hours after they had turned off the television set, the bedroom telephone rang and George Martin answered it in the dark. A desk sergeant's voice sounded unnecessarily loud.

"I guess you'd better get down here, Lieutenant. It's the rapist again."

"Same thing?"

"Worse this time. The victim's escort put up a fight. He's dead. Two bullets in his head."

George Martin look a long, deep breath. "Okay. In twenty minutes. Call out the lab men and Duffey and Hollister."

Alice Martin sat up in bed, switching on the bedlamp.

"Trouble?" she asked quietly.

"The worst. That rapist just became a murderer."

At headquarters Martin got the story quickly. At the edge of the city a hysterical girl had stumbled to the door of a suburban home to tell a startled couple about a man wearing a hood who had murdered her escort when the latter had tried to defend her.

"We've got her down in the infirmary. Doc Maguire is with her."

Martin took an elevator down and hurried to the infirmary. A girl who looked barely old enough to be out of high school was sitting in a white metal chair sipping nervously at a cup of coffee. She held it in both hands while an elderly police doctor leaned back against a table looking at her with heavy concentration. Martin glanced at the coffee, then gazed at the doctor with raised eyebrows.

"Sometimes coffee is as good as a sedative," Doc Maguire said. "Besides, Miss Odell has hold of herself now." He smiled at the girl and said, "This is Lieutenant Martin. He'll want to hear your story. Just take it easy now."

The doctor poured another cup of coffee from a glass coffee maker on a hot plate and handed it to Martin. "If you need me, I'll be in the other room."

Martin pulled up a chair and sat opposite the girl. For a few seconds they both sipped at coffee. The girl was holding herself under control only with an effort.

"Can you tell me about it now, Miss Odell?" he asked.

She put down her cup and nodded. "There's not much to tell. Bud—Bud Sherman, that was his name—Bud and I went to a show and then we went out and parked. It was really not what you may think. We were just good friends. He wasn't my boyfriend. I don't have one. I really didn't know him too well. Just a couple of dates."

"You've already told us what you know about Sherman?"

She nodded. "But you probably have to know how it happened."

"Yes."

"We'd been parked about fifteen minutes when a car passed us. We didn't think anything about it, but sat there looking down at the lights in the valley and just talking. Then this man suddenly appeared at the car door on Bud's side and put a gun against Bud's head. The man wore a hood. I screamed and he said for me to be quiet or he'd shoot."

"Would you recognize his voice?"

"I don't think so. He spoke very low."

"Then?"

"He told Bud to get out of the car. Bud backed out and for a minute the man lowered the gun when he sort of tripped as he backed up. He swore and Bud saw him stumble and turned and jumped at him. They fell to the ground and then there were two shots. Bud sort of slumped and the man in the hood got up and ran. I went to see if I could help Bud, but ..." She closed her eyes and Martin leaned forward to touch her hand.

"All right, Miss Odell. You don't need to go on."

She shook her head. "I saw that he was dead. I ran down the road a long ways until I saw a house with lights. I guess you know the rest." Her voice ended in a strangled sob.

"Would you recognize anything about the man?"

"No. He—he wore this hood thing over his head. It looked like the top of a woman's stocking."

"Could you see what his clothes were like?" Martin asked.

The girl thought for a moment. "He wore what looked like cheap cotton trousers. But there was something funny about his sport shirt under his jacket. It looked like the same material as his trousers."

"What color was the jacket?"

"Dark gray, I think."

"Did you notice anything else about him?"

"It all happened so fast, and they were fighting on the ground. He dropped something that looked like a blanket and picked it up before he ran."

"Which way did he run?"

The girl moistened her lips, then answered, still with a tremor in her voice. "Away from town. I heard a car start. I think he was parked up the road among the trees."

"All right," said Martin. "You'd probably like to go home. I'll have a car take you. Where do you live?"

"At the Y.W.C.A. I'm from out of town and work at an automobile finance company."

"Did your friend Bud have a family here?"

"No. He worked at the finance company, too. He was a collector. I think he came from South Dakota."

Martin thanked her and called into the other room for the doctor.

"Will you take care of her and see that she gets home, Doc? She lives at the Y.W."

The doctor nodded. "Your man Duffey just stuck his head in looking for you. He said he'd wait upstairs."

Martin went up to his office where Duffey and Hollister awaited him.

Duffey said, "A couple of men are out at the scene watching things. The lab men are downstairs."

"Let's go," Martin said crisply.

Two hours later Martin sat in his car, checking details with his two men. The gray light of dawn etched weariness in their faces and slowly transformed the wooded area into a dew-covered landscape.

Martin reviewed his notes. "The lab men found where his car was parked. The soil was wet enough for them to get a cast of tire marks, and that's the best thing we have."

"Footprints?" Duffey asked.

"Not good enough for a cast."

"They've got the bullets," Hollister said. "And two empty shells. Came from a thirty-two."

"No good unless we find the gun," Martin said. He gazed out across the valley. A uniformed man got in the dead man's car, turned it around and headed back to town with it. An ambulance had long since left with the body, and the lab men had finished their work and gone. There was nothing more to do here.

"The heat will be on," Martin said. "Horlick, the papers, the old man. They'll all be on our necks."

"I could take it better with some hot coffee under my belt," Duffey said.

Martin smiled crookedly. "Let's go find some. We'd better make it breakfast while we're at it. We may not get another chance for a while."

They drove back to town and selected an all night café and had breakfast. Their comments were almost desultory as they ate, and Martin was thoughtful. Within an hour or so he would be facing Chief Ansel and probably Cal Horlick.

There would be newspaper reporters, and conferences, and—if there was anything with which to work—leg work. He was not optimistic that anyone had seen the murderer drive away from the scene. No one had passed the girl as she walked for help. No gas stations were immediately beyond the scene on that little used road. He could send men out to ask questions, but he didn't expect any helpful answers.

Meanwhile the newspapers had the ingredients for a sensational story. The hood on the man was a natural for headlines. The repeated attacks that ended in murder all added up to front page, headline news. And all eyes would be turned upon the police department to do something about it. Actually, the attention would be focused upon one police lieutenant, George Martin.

Martin ordered a second cup of coffee and scowled at his two assistants.

"Do either of you have any ideas?"

Hollister said, "Only what we've already discussed. A tire mark isn't much to work with. And the description."

"Maybe there's something else," Martin said. "The Camman case."

Duffey's eyes narrowed thoughtfully. "Getting back to the first attack?"

"Think it over," Martin said. "In these car attacks it's been a hit or miss thing. I mean, the guy cruised around until he found a parked car. But in the Camman case he seems to have planned it. For one thing, he took his time. He wouldn't have unless he was sure he wasn't going to be disturbed. He knew Camman wouldn't be home, so he knew something about their habits, their time schedules."

Hollister nodded. "Makes sense."

Martin scowled. "And there's something else about that case that bothers me, but I can't put my finger on it." He finished his coffee and glanced at their empty cups. "Let's go face the wolves."

It was a little after seven o'clock when he entered headquarters again and he was notified that Chief Ansel wanted to see him. He went to the chief's office. Ansel sat behind his desk looking angry. Across from him Cal Horlick talked in a firm voice as Martin entered. Horlick broke off abruptly and turned to look at the detective.

"Hello, Martin. What have you got on it?"

Martin calmly crossed the room and sat in a chair.

"I'll tell you," he said quietly, and enumerated the facts that they had.

Horlick frowned. "Not much," he said. "What do you do next?"

Martin gazed at him steadily. "Go back to the Camman case," he said.

Horlick's lips tightened. "Why?"

"Because I think she knows more than she's told us, or because she's told us something and I've missed the significance of it."

"Then you've missed it," Horlick snapped.

Martin stood. "Is that all? If it is, I've work to do."

"That's all," Ansel said easily. "We'll have a conference later this morning."

Martin nodded curtly and left the office. He wondered why Horlick was so touchy about the Camman woman.

CHAPTER TWELVE
MILES SALIN

He hadn't meant to kill the man. Only it had happened so suddenly—his stumbling back and then the guy jumping him like that. Somehow the gun had come against the man's head and pulling the trigger had been automatic. Almost like snapping the shutter on a camera when you were ready to take a picture.

Now he was back in his room. This was the only familiar place of his own in the world. This room. He felt secure and hidden here. He had not turned on the light, but there was enough light sifting in from outside so that he could move about without running into things. Sitting on the edge of the bed, he stared straight ahead and tried to think what he should do.

For one thing he could get out of the jacket and coveralls. He could hide the rope and tape in the bottom drawer. Fold the blanket and put it at the foot of his bed; put away his camera and flash equipment. And he had better clean the gun.

The gun had been fully loaded and he had fired two shots. There would be two bullets missing and he had none to replace them. Miles doubted if anyone at the parking lot would ever check the gun. It hadn't been moved in the drawer since he had been there. He probably was safe enough about the missing bullets, but he'd have to wipe the gun handle when he put it back. Not that he couldn't explain prints on the gun, if it ever came to that. Anyone at the lot might handle the gun. Every employee had access to it in the drawer under the cash register.

He was sorry that he had killed the man, but he didn't feel sick about it. The man would have died sometime, anyhow. Everyone died sooner or later. What did it matter when you died?

If the guy had been sensible, he wouldn't have had to die this particular night. Nothing would have happened to him. He'd have been tied to a tree and a piece of tape would have been put over his mouth, and that was all. As a matter of fact, someone was probably doing him a favor, if he had only known it. Miles Salin was fixing things up for him.

The girl had looked like one of those prim and proper girls. She hadn't been necking with the guy. They had been sitting apart talking. Well, if the guy had behaved, Miles Salin would have fixed all that.

He'd have taken care of the girl—but good! He'd have taken plenty of pictures of her in poses that she wouldn't like so that she wouldn't have anything to hide any more. Yes, if that guy had behaved himself he'd have got his girl back. The guy was crazy. Instead of having that, he was dead.

Miles smiled in the darkness and was sorry that he hadn't had a chance to make love to the girl. She had been well built, too. It would have been nice to make her undress and do everything he told her to do.

He stood and put away the rope, tape, and gun. He unwrapped the camera and neatly folded the blanket and put it at the foot of the bed. He undressed then, glancing out the window once to check the bedroom window across the street. The window was dark.

In the morning he was awakened by Thelma's radio next door. The voice of a newscaster rattled through news events with a staccato pace broken only by the cheerful sound of a singing commercial.

Miles got up immediately. He had overslept a few moments and he would have to hurry. Thelma was moving about in her room, so he knew that the bathroom was unoccupied. He hurried down the hallway and shaved quickly.

By the time Thelma knocked on his door he was ready to leave. He came out into the hallway again with a smile.

"I had a swell sleep," he told her. "How about you?"

"Wonderful. But there was some terrible news this morning. Someone murdered a man in the hills in back of the Heights. They think it was that man who wears the hood and has been attacking girls up there. The parked car prowler."

"What happened?"

Briefly she told him the story as she had heard it from the newscast.

"Do they have any idea who the murderer is?" Miles asked.

"I guess not. One thing … we're certainly not going to do any parking out on dark roads."

He smiled. There it was again. That way she had of assuming that there was something solid and permanent between them—that he was her man.

Of course during the last few weeks she probably had enough reason in her own mind to believe that. They had been together often enough, and there had been the nights when she had come quietly to his room and left early in the morning.

There had been the pretext of taking pictures, and finally she had consented to pose in the nude for him, but as yet she hadn't. Maybe this would be a good night for that. He certainly wasn't going prowling tonight. The cops would be out in force. Couples would avoid parking in the hills.

He glanced at her and said, "Let's take some pictures tonight."

"What kind?"

"The ones we were talking about."

"Only if you promise that no one else will ever see them."

"Promise."

"Well, just a few then," she giggled, her eyes shining.

They stopped for breakfast at a cafe and, as he got out of the car, the gun in his inside coat pocket banged against the car door.

"You must have something awfully heavy in your pocket," Thelma said casually.

"I borrowed a pair of pliers from the lot," he said. He wondered what she would have said if she had known that it was the gun that had killed a man the night before. He'd be glad to get it back in the drawer, and he wished he had used the blackjack that he had fashioned weeks before.

Putting the gun back in the drawer had been easy. The lot was busy and he was alone in the shack when he opened the drawer. After carefully wiping the gun, he slipped it into the drawer. He felt easier as soon as he was rid of it.

Later in the morning he bought a newspaper and read the murder story. Obviously the cops had no lead and were trying desperately to find something.

"There isn't anything for them to find," he told himself. "But I'll have to be careful for a while."

That noon he ate at a drug store. When he came out Mary Jo Camman was walking on the sidewalk in front of him, returning to her office after lunch. He remembered when he had followed her before, and the things he had learned about her and her husband.

Now he walked behind her and he remembered how it had been with her. This noon she wore a skirt, sweater, and short jacket. The skirt was tight across her buttocks and it excited him to watch her walk and to observe the play of her body beneath the close-fitting cloth.

It gave him a sense of pleasure to know that he had once possessed this woman—that he was as familiar with her body as a man could possibly be. Yet if she stopped and turned and looked at him, she would not know him.

A sudden, intense desire drew a ruddy veil across his eyes and he spoke silently to himself: "You bitch ... I've had you. I made you like it."

The quick wave of overpowering desire passed, but left a deeper urge to possess her once more. It was good enough with Thelma, and it had been satisfying with the girls in the woods, but nothing compared with the way it had been with this woman when he had plenty of time and she was powerless to stop him.

Ahead of him Mary Jo turned into the office building where she worked. Miles walked on past and circled the block toward the parking lot. The hot, trembling, intense feeling was in his groin, and he was restless so that he felt that same need again. Tonight he'd be with Thelma. Maybe they'd make love, maybe they'd take some pictures—maybe they'd do both.

He glanced at the late afternoon headlines. No arrest had been made. Couples were urged not to park on lonely roads. Night police patrols were being increased. He smiled at one headline: MURDER THOUGHT WORK OF MADMAN. Let them think that. Then they'd never suspect him!

CHAPTER THIRTEEN
MARY JO CAMMAN

"But weren't you frightened?" Carrie Gould asked her. Carrie was a dark, vivacious woman with a petite body that was almost doll-like in its proportions.

"I am now," Mary Jo admitted. She finished putting dishes away in a cupboard in the large kitchen of the old house and sat at the table where Carrie watched her. Full coffee cups were there for them and a half pot of coffee still was warm on the stove.

Bill Camman and Al Gould had gone bowling for the evening and the couple had eaten together. Mary Jo was glad that she had company for the evening. The late editions of the papers still headlined the murder of the previous evening.

She crossed the kitchen and sat at the table with the other woman. The night before they finally had discussed what had happened to her. Al had told Carrie, of course, and the murder had led them into the subject at dinner. Now, however, was the first time that the two women had been alone to talk and Mary Jo knew that Carrie was curious.

Carrie said, "Can you talk about it, Mary Jo?"

"I suppose it's silly not to talk about it with your best friend," Mary Jo smiled thinly. "It's not as if we were innocent little high school girls—if there are any these days."

Carrie nodded thoughtfully and said, "Mary Jo … has it made a difference between you and Bill?"

"Why do you ask that?"

"The little we talked about it last night. It was the dark, brooding look that came over Bill's face."

"So you noticed it, too."

"So did Al. It bothered us."

Mary Jo studied her friend's face and saw concern and sympathy there.

"It's made a difference," she admitted.

"But that's unfair! It wasn't your fault."

"He knows all that, Carrie. And he's really never said anything. It's just that things have been different since. I don't believe he can help it."

"Do you feel any different, Mary Jo?"

"I suppose so. Things like that can't happen to you without making a difference."

"It must have been terrible. How could Bill ever think that you ... well, that you might have been enjoying it or anything!"

"I don't know that he does," Mary Jo said, remembering that he did and knowing that she lied. "I don't believe it's that."

Carrie was about to say something, then stopped with a queer expression on her face.

"But you *could* have," she said, almost to herself.

"Do you think you could?" Mary Jo asked her.

Carrie returned her stare with complete candor. "I'll be perfectly honest with you, Mary Jo. Maybe I couldn't help myself. I'm that way about sex. Al could never accuse me of being frigid. And I hate the false modesty some women have about admitting that they like sex. I do, Mary Jo. And I'm not sure I could ever just turn it off once a man had started with me ... no matter who he might be." She laughed a trifle self-consciously. "We've hardly ever mentioned this before, I guess! But sex is such a natural thing, and it's so much a part of us. Are you that way, Mary Jo?"

"I suppose so," Mary Jo replied guardedly.

"So if you got a … well, a *thrill* out of it … you couldn't help it."

"You make it sound almost clinical, Carrie."

"It is … almost. Anyhow, Bill probably thinks you got something out of it in spite of yourself, and men are so possessive. Al is. He knows that Lannie Minters and I were engaged in school and he brings it up every once in a while. Trying to find out how far Lannie and I went."

Mary Jo listened to Carrie with a full understanding of her. She had known Carrie since they were in grade school, and they had lived in the same block. She knew Carrie's insatiable curiosity, and her interest in men, and sex, and sexual affairs. But Carrie already had said enough about this and what had happened. She decided to forestall further questioning.

"Well, how far *did* you and Lannie go? You never told me."

"Further than I'll ever tell Al!" Carrie giggled. "But this really scares me about you, Mary Jo. Since he killed that man. Think what might have happened to you!"

"He hasn't hurt any women. But I suppose he could."

"And those terrible photographs. Honestly, Mary Jo—he really didn't take any of you?"

"No, Carrie."

"Weren't you worried about becoming pregnant?"

"For a while."

"That probably worried Bill, too."

Mary Jo got up and took the empty coffee cups to the sink. She knew that Carrie had dozens of questions that she wanted to ask, and she understood Carrie well enough not to be angry. But she didn't want to talk about it any more. Carrie had edged too close to a truth that she didn't want to admit even to herself.

And there had been the dreams. Each time there had been the stranger and he had taken her. The dreams had been so intense that they had awakened her.

But Carrie was right about the way Bill sometimes looked at her. Things were different between them. Although he had made love to her finally, it had been a different kind of love and she had felt his abnormal excitement and resented it.

She washed the cups and left them on the drainboard. Dusk had fallen and she turned on the kitchen light. For a moment she was at a loss to know what to do with Carrie. The things they usually talked about seemed unimportant, and she knew that Carrie still was curious.

"There's some good TV," she suggested.

Carrie nodded indifferently and got up and filled one of the coffee cups and took it back to the table. "I'd like some more coffee first," she said. She sipped it tentatively and put the cup down. "Mary Jo, what did he do? What did he *really* do?"

Mary Jo saw the animated interest in Carrie's eyes, the probing for facts and vicarious details, and suddenly she resented it. Yet, simultaneously, she felt a vicious impulse to shock Carrie.

She poured more coffee for herself and returned to the table. "All right, Carrie, I'll tell you. But you're not to tell Al. Will you promise that?"

"Of course!"

"Then this is what happened ..." Slowly and in detail she described the love-making to which she had been subjected, for some reason getting a satisfaction in seeing the growing excitement and shock in Carrie's eyes.

Suddenly, however, Mary Jo's own mood changed and she realized that the telling had become a welcome cathartic of her emotions.

She stopped speaking for a moment and thought, *This thing that happened to me is probably no different from what many women have experienced by their own invitation, or even in the normality of marriage … maybe weekly … time after time.*

Abruptly she smiled and said, "Carrie, stop looking that way. There really was nothing so terrible about it except the ropes, the tape, the blindfold and the sense of helplessness. That made it different. What happened to me has happened to thousands of women. "I simply got laid."

"Mary Jo! Why that's—that's an awful thing to say!"

"Why? You were telling me just a while ago that you enjoy sex. Well, I do, too. Not that way—not tied and gagged and blindfolded with a man I don't know who's doing whatever he pleases with me. But nothing really devastating or earth-shaking happened to me. I was had. As far as that goes, Lannie Minters probably laid you when we were in school. But no one is making a big fuss about it."

Carrie's eyes were round and wide with shock. "I never heard you talk like this, Mary Jo!" she said with considerable vehemence.

"I know," Mary Jo said, almost wearily. "But maybe I'm just being matter-of-fact and talking the way both of us actually think. At least, it's the way Bill sometimes talked before this happened. Men have a way of putting things in down-to-earth language. But women seem to think they have to keep it under wraps. And this once I won't."

Now Carrie was smiling a little. "I think I know what you mean. If Bill could look at it this way …"

"Most men can't under these circumstances. A man might marry a girl who had had three husbands previously, and that would be all right. But the same man would think the world had come to an end if—well, if something like this happened to his wife." Mary Jo took a sip of her coffee and put the cup down again. "I'm glad we've had this talk. I feel better now."

Carrie leaned forward. "But what are you going to do about Bill?"

"Wait ... and hope, I guess."

"Aren't the police afraid that man will come back here again?" Carrie asked, glancing instinctively at the door. "Isn't that what you said the lieutenant told you last night?"

"That was last night. I don't know now. Bill thinks the man probably left town after last night."

"Doesn't it worry you?"

"Of course, I'm frightened. Yet what Bill says sounds right. You wouldn't think he'd take a chance."

"He might come back if—" Carrie hesitated and appeared startled by her own thoughts. "Mary Jo, there isn't any reason why he might think you could identify him, is there?"

"No. If that has bothered him, he—" Mary Jo understood Carrie's meaning and her eyes widened a little. "He's a murderer now. If I *could* identify him ..."

"You'd be in terrible danger if he thought you could."

Mary Jo suppressed a shudder. "We're sitting here imagining things, Carrie. Let's go and watch TV. I'm certain there's no danger."

They went into the living room and turned on the set. It was a relief to hear the voice of a comedian and the cheerfulness of music and Mary Jo felt herself relax.

At ten o'clock she got up to put coffee on again. They expected Bill and Al back from the bowling alleys before long and she had sandwiches and pie ready in the refrigerator. Carrie went upstairs to the bathroom and in a few moments Mary Jo joined her.

Carrie wanted to see the new spreads Mary Jo had bought and they chatted in the bedroom for a few moments. Carrie sat on the edge of a bed facing the window and occasionally she glanced outside.

"I wonder what that is," she finally said.

"What?" Mary Jo turned to look out the window.

"In that big house over there. The lighted window where the shade is drawn. There! See how the light got strong behind the blind. In a few moments it will grow weaker."

Mary Jo watched the change. "That's odd. I never noticed that before. What do you suppose it is?"

"Maybe someone is fooling with a lamp or something."

"A lamp wouldn't be that strong."

A door opened downstairs and Bill's voice sounded up the stairwell.

"They're home," Mary Jo said. The two women went into the hallway and toward the stairs. "Carrie ..." Mary Jo spoke softly. "Please don't repeat any of our conversation to Al. You know what I mean."

Carrie smiled almost guiltily. "Don't worry! I might start those questions about Lannie Minters again, and I'd just as soon not talk about *that!*"

CHAPTER FOURTEEN
CAL HORLICK

Alone in his apartment on the Heights, Cal Horlick poured himself a drink and put a symphony on the hi-fi set he recently had installed. The music sounded full-bodied and rich and he sat in an easy chair and savored the taste of the twelve-year-old Scotch.

This was not a bad life he had cut out for himself, he reflected. The ambitions he had set for himself long ago were beginning to materialize. Already he had been approached about the coming election and assured that he could be the next D.A.

A good, fighting D.A. could lead to the governor's mansion and on to the Senate. Or he could direct his course toward some big industrial outfit where he could command a high salary. Sometimes he was not quite sure which was more important to him—power or money.

"Both," he told himself. "But one at a time. One brings the other."

He thought about the rapist and murderer. This was a case made to order for him—if the police could catch up with the man. Even if they didn't, it gave him an opportunity for head-lines in criticizing the department. Either way a man could use it to build himself a little more as a hero in the public eye. This case even had an element of personal interest that he normally failed to find.

A good many years had passed since he had thought much about Mary Jo. Meeting her again and finding her involved in the case had hit him with surprising impact.

For one thing, Mary Jo had become a woman. Her immaturity of that summer at the beach had been replaced with a rich fullness of femininity that was altogether startling. More than that, she had reawakened his desire for her.

He shut his eyes and remembered her as a girl in her teens and the intensity of his own sensual yearnings when he had been in her company. He still felt chagrined when he recalled how his own youthful inexperience and impatience had proved his undoing.

He smiled a little as he remembered the old saw: "… it isn't the ones that you had that you remember so much—it's the ones you could have had and didn't."

Well, she had been had. Drastically so, not too long ago. The crime itself filled him with anger and disgust, but he recognized the transient elements involved.

Mary Jo had not been physically injured, but he wondered about her psychologically. Bill Camman, her husband, did not impress him especially. A run-of-the-mill newspaperman with a wire service. Probably a confused man since this had happened to his wife.

In a way, it was strange that Mary Jo had married a man like that. She had the qualities that could have brought her a better marriage.

Abruptly he thought of his morning review of the case with Chief Ansel. The murder now was four days old and the department had failed to make any significant progress.

"I want some kind of protection for Mrs. Camman," Cal had insisted. "That murderer's a psycho. He could get ideas about her again."

"She's getting protection," Ansel had told him. "Martin's arranged it. Tonight Camman works until after midnight and we've got a car in the neighborhood. Also she's been instructed to leave lights burning all over the house and on the porch."

Horlick glanced at his watch. It was shortly after nine o'clock and Mary Jo was probably alone. Acting upon impulse, he got up and went to a telephone. He found the Camman number and dialed it. Her voice sounded strangely familiar after all the years.

"Cal Horlick," he told her. "I was thinking about you. Chief Ansel told me you'd be alone tonight, but that they're checking the neighborhood. Is everything all right?"

"I'm all right, Cal. Maybe a little nervous, but I'm sure there's no reason why I should be."

"Would it be all right if I stopped by for a moment? I'd like to check some details with you."

He realized that he had nothing to check, but the thought had been as impulsive as his calling her.

"I'd like some company," she said. "I'll put coffee on."

"In twenty minutes or so," he told her and hung up.

On the way there Cal avoided thinking what had prompted the call. He could rationalize it if he wished, but he knew that it would be rationalization. He simply had a desire to see Mary Jo Camman. He could talk about the case. He could find details to check with her. It would be better, anyhow, if someone were with her.

In the neighborhood he cruised until he spotted a prowl car and pulled up alongside it. The officers recognized him.

"I'm going to Camman's place," he informed them. "Thought I'd better check with you so you'll know who's parked there."

He left them and drove to the old house. Mary Jo came to the door dressed in sweater and skirt and he was even more conscious of the transformation from girl to woman that had taken place.

"Come in, Hal," she smiled. "I'm glad you stopped by."

He shed his light topcoat and hat and she took him to the living room, excused herself, and returned with coffee.

"I should have asked you if you'd rather have a drink," she apologized. "We have some Bourbon, I think."

"No. Just the coffee." He sipped at it tentatively and smiled at her. "I think we're old enough friends for me to tell you that you look lovely, Mary Jo." His glance appraised her figure warmly.

"Thank you, Cal." She smiled back at him. "You've grown up, too. Why did you really come here tonight?"

"I never did fool you much. Even when we were kids."

"We weren't so much kids as inexperienced. Do you really have some details to clear up?"

"I have some questions. Somehow, though, they're not entirely pertinent to finding the murderer."

"Then what?"

"About you."

"Do we want to talk about that, Cal?"

He put his cup down and offered her a cigarette, lighting one for himself when she refused.

"I'd like it," he said. "I've wondered how it has been with you, how your married life has been, how life has treated you?"

"Why are you so interested now?"

"For one thing, we might have been married, Mary Jo. For another, I've never met another woman who interested me."

"Yes, we might have been married," she said, and there was a quixotic amusement in her eyes. "But we didn't, and now I'm married and satisfied with my marriage. Does that answer some of it for you?"

"Not entirely."

She gazed at him seriously and there was an amused candor in her voice when she spoke.

"Tell me something, Cal. When a man knows that a woman has been raped, does that make her more desirable, or a possible conquest?"

"That's a hell of a question!" His face flushed and a flicker of annoyance darkened his eyes.

"It's an honest one. I think it even may have something to do with your being here tonight."

"I wanted you long before you were raped—or married. You know that damned well."

She nodded and smiled again. "Is that why you stopped writing to me? Were you so embarrassed about the whole thing?"

"Truthfully I don't know," he said. She was surprising him with her bluntness, but not unpleasantly. This attitude erased a good many years between them and brought them to a compatible level. "Undoubtedly that was some of it," he said, "and then I became interested in what I was going to do with my life. I began to develop ambitions. I probably became entirely self-centered for a time."

"You're not now?" There was a light, teasing note in Mary Jo's voice.

"Enough to know where I'm going, and to know that I'm going to get there," Cal retorted.

"Hasn't there been a girl?"

"Not seriously."

"One day on the street you said something that sounded as if you wanted me to think that you still are in love with me. I didn't believe it, Cal. I don't now."

"This conversation is moving pretty fast, isn't it?" he grinned.

Mary Jo shook her head. "No. It's a sort of self defense upon my part."

"I don't understand."

"Since the attack—let's be frank again—since the rape, my husband seems to be suspicious of me and my best friend is secretly convinced that I enjoyed it. Now my first love—and you were my first love, you know—comes around again with thinly disguised passes."

For an instant Cal was thoroughly enraged until he realized that she had come closer to the truth than was comfortable.

"I'm sorry if you think I'm making passes," he said.

"That's the assistant D.A. speaking," she laughed lightly. "A good politician never sticks his neck out, does he, Cal? But you're safe. Really you are. It's between you and me."

She stopped talking for half a moment, then looked into his eyes with a quizzical expression.

"I don't know why I'm talking this way," she admitted. "Unless I feel as if I've been cornered and have to fight back."

"You don't have to fight me, Mary Jo."

"I know that. What we had a long time ago was really pretty strong, Cal. You could have had me once."

"But not now," he said.

Her eyes widened a trifle. "I'm not sure. I'm not sure of anything about myself any more. Six weeks ago I'd have been shocked to even think about it. But remember—I was raped and I'm finding out a few things that the experience does to other people besides yourself."

"It doesn't have to be that important," he said. "I don't mean that I'm dismissing the gravity of the crime against you, Mary Jo. But it's only really going to damage you if it damages you psychologically."

"Isn't that sometimes the worst kind of damage?"

"Yes," he admitted.

"Tell me this, Cal. Were you going to tell me that you still love me? You've acted that way. You did that day on the street."

"I think I do."

"No. I don't believe you do. I think it's because you could have had me once, and you didn't get me. It's unfinished business."

He thought, *you remember the ones you could have had and didn't.* She could be very right. He forced a smile and shrugged.

"I'm no match for you tonight, Mary Jo. Maybe I never was."

She laughed again, the light amused laugh. "Cal, I don't love you. Sometimes I've wondered how it would have been if we had married, but I don't love you."

"There's been no reason why you should."

"No, there's no reason why I should. Do you want more coffee?"

He shook his head and put out his cigarette. "There's one thing we can talk about," he said. "The danger you may be in. I want you to be very careful until we pick up this man."

"I suppose he *could* come back. But it seems so improbable, Cal."

"Not if he …" He hesitated, and then shrugged. "To be as frank as you've been, it's not improbable if he enjoyed you. We have every reason to think he's a psycho. If the desire is great enough, nothing else will matter much to him. Could you tell if—?"

"He enjoyed himself," she said flatly.

"I'm not sure I like having you here alone. How late does Bill work on nights like this?"

"He usually gets home a little after two in the morning."

"And you go to bed?"

"Sometimes. Sometimes I stay up."

"Can you lock your bedroom door?"

"I don't know. I hadn't thought about it. It seems so … well, like locking Bill out of his bedroom. He'd have to awaken me to get in."

"Let's take a look at the door, anyhow."

"If you like." She got up and led the way upstairs and they inspected the bedroom door lock.

"An ordinary skeleton key from a dime store would handle it," he said, frowning. "These old locks. You could have Bill put a bolt on it."

"Cal, I think all this is unnecessary. The police go by frequently when he's working, and I keep the lights on. Besides they should get the man soon. Shouldn't they?"

"I hope so." He looked around the bedroom, at the beds, and realized that this was where the attack had taken place. "Which is your bed?"

She glanced at him almost sharply and said, "The one nearest the window. The scene of the crime … if that's what you want to know."

A warm tide of blood reddened his face at her words. "Don't forget that law enforcement is part of my job," he reminded her crisply. "I've never been up here before, and I'm curious from a professional viewpoint."

"I'm sorry, Cal. You probably are. Only the police have been over and over it all."

He walked to the window near the bed and looked out. Autumn leaves had begun to fall, but he saw that the room still was protected from the street by foliage. Across the street one window was visible. A dim light filtered from it through a drawn blind.

"Do you always leave the blind up?" he asked.

"I suppose so. No one can see in."

"Did you that night?"

"Yes ... I'm sure because the man pulled it down. I remember that."

A vague idea began to press at the back of Cal's mind. Perhaps, it was only one chance in a thousand, but in a case like this every idea might be important.

"Mary Jo, I want you to think back and tell me exactly what you did before you went to sleep that evening."

She sensed the seriousness of his voice.

"I'll try to remember," she said. "First I came upstairs and decided to take a shower."

"Wait. Did you undress here?"

"Yes. I'd been sunbathing and I had on shorts and a halter. I took them off here in the bedroom and then had my shower and came back."

"Then what did you do?"

"I think I stood in front of the mirror for a few moments and checked my tan. I suppose everyone does."

"As I recall from the report, it was dark outside by then. Did you have the light on?"

"Yes."

"And you were in the nude?"

She nodded.

"Then you stretched out on the bed, didn't you?" he asked.

"There was a cool breeze. So I cooled off for a little while."

"No clothes?"

"I didn't have anything on. After a while I got drowsy and pulled the spread over me."

"And when you awoke he was here."

She nodded again. "Why, Cal? You act as if you've thought of something, or found something."

He looked at her thoughtfully. "Whoever it was must have known that you were here alone—here in this room. It was all too well planned."

"Lieutenant Martin thought that, too."

Cal indicated the window. "There's one place from where you were visible. From that room across the street. As nearly as I can determine, it's the only place."

"But could anyone actually see in? Isn't the bed too low?"

"Let's see. Stretch out on the bed and I'll sight from the other side of the bed. I'll put out the light to make it easier to line up the light in that window."

Silently she went to the bed and lay on her back. The attorney knelt and sighted. He stood and went to the bed and sat on the edge of it, by her in the darkness.

"The bed is completely visible from that window," he said.

She was completely motionless and didn't answer him. He sensed rather than saw that her eyes were closed.

"Is anything wrong?" he asked quietly.

"I don't know," she said softly. "Oh, nothing at the moment. I mean, right now about what you've been asking. But this is where it happened, with my eyes closed like this, and—Cal, I want an answer. Maybe I'll never have another chance to find out for myself."

Her hands found his arms and pulled him gently so that he bent over her and a small pulse began to beat in his throat. His hands found her and the palms slid beneath her shoulders and he felt her arms pull him down to her. Her lips were soft and moist and opened to his kiss.

She pushed him away with sudden violence. He immediately released her and tried to quiet the emotional storm that she had awakened in him.

"I'm sorry," he said in the dark.

"It wasn't your fault, Cal," she told him, her voice weak. They got up from the bed and she passed him and went into the hallway as he turned on the light.

"Was there a reason for that?" he asked.

"Yes. I wanted an answer."

"Did you get it?"

"Yes."

"Do you want to tell me, Mary Jo?"

"I don't have to tell you. You know the answer. Please, let's go downstairs," She sounded perturbed.

They went down to the living room and she brought hot coffee to them. This time she accepted a cigarette.

"Does all that about the window mean anything, Cal?" she asked.

"Who lives in that house?"

"It's a rooming house, but Lieutenant Martin checked everyone there."

"I think we'd better check it again. It's a slim chance, but it's worth it."

"I'm certain you won't find anything," she said.

He dismissed her doubts with a small gesture and met her eyes with a steady gaze.

"When I came in, you said something about our being 'grown up' and adult. Does that give us the right to discuss something as adults, Mary Jo?"

"I suppose it does."

"You didn't want me to stop up there, did you?"

"No, I didn't. Is that what you want to know?"

"One of the things. And I'd like to know why."

"That's a fair question, but I'm not going to answer it."

"Because there still is something left from that summer?"

"Listen to me, Cal. I'm married. I love Bill. I wouldn't have married him unless I loved him. But now I'm not sure how I love him. Can you understand that?"

"Yes."

"Do you want to know if I would go to bed with you? Is that it?"

"Stop talking like that. It isn't you."

"Oh, yes it is. These are some of the psychological things you talked about. Remember?"

"All right, if you want to call spades spades … I want to go to bed with you. I wanted to that night on the beach. Too much. I lost my chance, and I've never stopped wanting to go to bed with you since. And after tonight I know something else. I want to marry you."

"I'm married."

"I know that, too."

"There isn't anything I can do about that. I don't think I'd want to do anything about it. You don't know how it has been with Bill and me. You don't know about the things that go into building a marriage—the troubles you share, the pain you experience and the ambitions you try to achieve. The private little jokes you have between you, and the special married language you speak together."

"All right," he said, almost angrily. "I don't. I haven't been married. But you wanted to be loved up there. Deny that."

"That's what I'm talking about, Cal. You don't know anything above love. Listen to me. I didn't want to be loved. I wanted to be laid. Is that plain enough? I wanted to be had. I wanted you to take me. And it didn't have anything to do with love as Bill and I know it, nor as you and I might have known it, nor as it's talked about by the people who are supposed to know. That's what rape did to me. And that's what I found out up there. Now get out of here, Cal."

He took a deep, quivering breath and returned her stare. He sensed what she was trying to say, and he knew, too, that there was an honest confusion in her mind so that she wasn't sure about herself. He also understood her desperate attempt to clarify her thinking with this cold and literal talk.

"Not this way, Mary Jo," he said. "You're overlooking that we're friends. Maybe that's the most important thing."

Suddenly her high emotion was gone and she had closed her eyes. After a moment she shook her head a little and smiled.

"I'm sorry, Cal. Truly I am."

"It's all right. Can we talk about it later?"

"Maybe we had better. It can't be left in mid-air."

"Good. Then I'll leave now and let you get some sleep. Pull that blind upstairs. And don't be alarmed if you hear a car park outside. I'm going to have that prowl car stay out there until Bill comes home."

CHAPTER FIFTEEN
BILL CAMMAN

Max Sinto left his desk in the city room and crossed to the large, glassed-in office rented from the newspaper by the wire service. He felt his usual impatience with Saturday night dullness at the newspaper, but there was at least some variety this night and he approached Bill Camman almost tentatively.

Bill looked up from his typewriter. "Slow night," he said.

Sinto pulled up a battered office chair and sat down. "I've a problem, Bill."

"Can I help you?"

Sinto shrugged. "One of the crime mags wants a complete story on the murder."

"I suppose so," Bill said. "The sex and murder angle."

"I can make some dough with it, but I don't like to do the story. It means involving your wife."

Bill carefully finished typing the last of a story he was rewriting for the radio wire and pulled the paper from his machine. He had been worrying about this and Max Sinto's words came as no surprise to him.

"Someone is going to write it, Max. I'd rather have you handle it than a lot of other guys."

"They might go for a fictitious name."

"I don't know. Everyone in town will figure it out, anyhow. But the fictitious name might help."

"And they might not. If you'd rather I tried to kill the story, I will. Just say the word."

"You couldn't kill it. They'd probably send someone in to cover it. You'd better take the assignment."

"Okay. I'll do the story. But work with me and maybe we can keep the stuff about your wife toned down."

"I'll help you all I can. Wire them that you'll cover the story, Max. You may as well get the dough as anyone."

"I'll get a wire off then. You had coffee yet?"

"I think I'll wait a while."

Sinto nodded and left. Bill watched the retreating, rotund figure of the man and lit a cigarette. Now he fully understood for the first time the resentment that people could feel toward the press. He could logically condone the efforts of publishers to print the news. He himself was a part of the news industry and his livelihood depended upon the things that happened to other people. But now he felt the same resentment that so many of them had shown toward the invasion of privacy in his life and home.

Because it was second nature for him to interpret his thoughts and the events of living into written words, he automatically saw his own words in print, and he knew that his story would be drastically different from the one Max Sinto would eventually write.

It was all a matter of viewpoint. Max Sinto's viewpoint would be that of the newsman—objective, reportorial, factual. Mary Jo would have a viewpoint—the victim, soiled ... the principal. Yes, even the rapist would have a viewpoint—possibly justifying his crimes, or flaunting them. None of these constituted Bill Camman's viewpoint. Impulsively Bill put a fresh sheet of paper in his machine and typed rapidly:

"I am the husband of a woman who was raped.

"On a late Saturday night when I was at work, an unidentified man crept into my house, attacked my wife, defiled her, and in one act, covering a relatively few moments in our lives, he changed a marriage, changed a woman, and changed a man.

"Never again can I look at my wife in the secure knowledge that ..."

He stopped typing and scanned the lines he had written. In an angry gesture he snatched the paper from the machine, tore it into bits, and dropped it into a waste basket.

"You've got to get yourself squared around on this," he told himself bitterly. "It wasn't Mary Jo's fault. She didn't go out and make a play for another man. She didn't even have a chance to defend herself."

He knew the futility of telling himself this, because he had said it over and over to himself, recognizing the truth of it, and trying desperately to adjust himself to the facts.

He prided himself upon being an intelligent man, believing that his background and the very nature of his work must necessarily contribute to intelligence.

He believed that he was tolerant, and not too easily shocked. He readily forgave many transgressions in others because from the news side of life he had learned to expect transgressions and had come to understand many of the reasons for them.

He had worked with several men who had been married yet who had gone with prostitutes or had had affairs with other women, and he had accepted those conditions with matter-of-fact understanding.

He had known women who would sleep with virtually anyone, and liked them nonetheless for it. He had felt sympathy for murderers because he could understand the drives and impulses that had brought them to the point of killing.

He had learned to accept the world and life and people at face value, never expecting too much, never believing that some things could never happen, and never too critical of anything or anyone. He had been trained in objectivity and tried to live by his training.

The breakdown of this self-styled intelligence and sympathy bothered him in itself—beyond the natural reactions that he believed a man should experience when his wife had been violated.

Trying to fathom his frustrations about it, Bill wondered how pertinent it was that he had never made love to any woman other than his wife.

Despite his small show of worldly wisdom, he had been singularly inexperienced with girls before he had met and married Mary Jo. There had been a dual loss of virginities upon their wedding night and he had been forced to rely for guidance upon the books he had read before the marriage, and one brief talk with his physician.

From this preparation he had approached the wedding night with great caution and an alertness for pain and emotional reaction from Mary Jo.

He had steeled himself to be gentle and considerate. He was certain that Mary Jo would find no pleasure in that first night, for the books had forewarned him.

He recognized the possibility that Mary Jo might not experience the full delights of their union during the first few weeks of their marriage. This, too, had been stated in the books. Thus, in tremenduous excitement and with deep apprehension he had approached Mary Jo in the sterile strangeness of the dark hotel room.

The books had been right to this degree: there was Mary Jo's one small cry of pain. But it was followed almost immediately by an enthusiasm and abandon from her that left him spent and exhausted before he realized what had happened. She held him to her tightly, laughing softly and murmuring, "Oh, darling ... darling ... darling ... it's so good!"

Somehow he managed to smile at himself and remember that the books had said 'in many cases'—and he had never suspected that Mary Jo might be an exception to the many cases of pain and temporary disillusion.

"You're sure?" he had whispered. "You're not lying to make me feel all right about it?"

"Oh, Bill!" Darling! It was wonderful! But I guess your girl is just lucky." She moved close to him, and her lips played at his throat beneath his chin. "Do we have to wait long?" she whispered. "I want to again ..."

Remembering as he sat at his typewriter, Bill realized that this was an invasion of privacy that a rapist had made. This was something that had belonged to Mary Jo and him, and had been stolen. Mary Jo had not given it. It had been stolen, changed, scarred, made strangely different.

Now Mary Jo knew another man, and the word *knew* took on a new significance for him. For a woman must certainly know a man when he was taking her; know the feel of him and his strength and his love-making in detail.

"God damn it!" Bill muttered savagely. "God damn the bastard!"

What other man had a right to enter Mary Jo? To take her—to bring her to the abandonment of climax and ecstasy! Bill swore softly and steadily in a vicious yielding to anger and frustration. Finally he stood and walked away from the machine, fighting for control of his outraged feelings. There was nothing he could do about it now. The deed was done. It could not be erased.

Nor must he let himself be victimized again by his own unexpected and unexplainable curiosity about what had actually happened to her that night. In the undefinable feeling of possession that he experienced for her there had been an insistent desire to know exactly what she had endured.

But the passion her words had aroused, the imagined pictures they had conjured up, had inspired in him an almost perverted desire to punish her, to take her, to obliterate the memory of another man from her by the sheer and brutal force of his own manhood.

Bill had tried to analyze it thus afterwards, but he was not certain that he had. He had felt a measure of shame, not only for the violence with which he had taken Mary Jo, but for the reasons that had inspired his sensual outburst.

He glanced at the electric clock in the city room. It was almost eleven. He would be home with Mary Jo in a little more than three hours.

Certain that she would not be sleeping, he dialed their number and the sound of her voice was strangely reassuring.

"Just checking, honey," he told her. "Everything all right?"

"Fine! I've been watching TV. Cal Horlick stopped by for a little while and then made arrangements for a police car to park out front. I think it's sort of silly, but he insisted. So you won't have to worry. They'll stay until you get home."

"Why? Has something broken on the case?"

"No ... nothing new."

"But why did he stop by?"

"Probably because I've known him for years, as he told you. We visited a while and he checked upstairs."

"What for?"

"He wanted to be sure that I could lock the bedroom door if I had to. Then he noticed a window in Mrs. Lindicott's rooming house. I guess we'd better pull the blind after this."

"Are the cops out in front now?"

"They were a few moments ago and I haven't heard a car start."

"I'll be home as soon as I get through. I'm glad the cops are there. I'll feel better. You're sure you're all right?"

"Certainly I am, darling," Mary Jo assured him. "I'll wait up until you get home and I'll have coffee and sandwiches ready. Don't worry. If I get frightened I'll call you—but I don't think I will with the police at our front door!"

He laughed at his own apprehension. "Okay. I'll bring them in for a cup of coffee and something to eat when I get home. Have plenty of stuff ready."

He hung up and stared at the phone for a moment, then dialed police headquarters, identified himself, and asked for the detective bureau. He repeated his identification for the detective who answered. "Just wondering if anything new has broken on the case," he said.

"Nothing," the detective told him. "We've got a car out at your place, though, so you don't have to worry, Mr. Camman."

"My wife told me. I appreciate it. Just made me wonder if something is up."

"No. Just precautions. We'll give you a ring if anything new comes in."

Bill returned to his desk and lit a cigarette. Well, Max might cover the story, but there was one thing he couldn't have. There would be no picture of Mary Jo. No picture for men and women all over the country to study as they told themselves: "This woman was raped."

CHAPTER SIXTEEN
THELMA JORGSON

Thelma stared at the pictures Miles Salin showed her. They were in his room late this Saturday night. She wore a housecoat that was obviously her only garment. Miles wore an old pair of blues and a white T-shirt. They had just returned from the darkroom and Thelma was looking at enlargements of the nude studies Miles recently had taken of her.

"Oh! I'm embarrassed!" she said and a deep blush spread from her neck up to her face.

"You shouldn't be," he told her. "You're beautiful, Thelma."

"But I look … the pictures make me look so *abandoned*. Did you deliberately pose me that way, Miles?" There was an edge to her voice.

"It was an accident," Miles said and she thought she detected a slight evasiveness in the way he spoke.

"If I thought you did it deliberately—"

"Look, Thelma, I didn't. After all, you are … well, you're seductive. I don't see anything wrong with these pictures. They're good art studies."

She sifted through the small pile, studying each picture with a quick glance, the blush on her cheeks growing constantly deeper. She put them down on a table and looked at him.

"Please, Miles … destroy them. The negatives, too. I'd simply die if anyone else ever saw them!"

"No one ever will, Thelma. I promise you. And you haven't anything to be ashamed of. These are really art studies. I don't believe you've ever seen the other kind, have you?"

She saw the glint of excitement in his eyes as he glanced at her. Suddenly she was apprehensive. Not that she was prudish. She hardly could be, working in the office of a gynecologist and after her affair with Dan who had gone to Alaska, and then with Miles. Actually, she supposed, the studies of her in the nude were not in bad taste. They were—as he had worded it—seductive, and she was not certain that she had not intended them to be when she had posed for him.

The small admission of guilt to herself brought a smile. "Well, I probably did pose that way for you. And I'm certain they're not like the other kind, although I've never seen any of those."

He studied her a moment with an air of indecision. Finally he shook his head and said, "No, you'd probably get the wrong idea about me."

"Wrong idea about what, Miles?"

"Skip it."

Now her curiosity was aroused and she became persuasive. "Please, Miles. What?"

"You know what pornography is?"

"Certainly."

"It's quite a study. I read somewhere that Dr. Kinsey's assistants have been conducting a comprehensive survey on the subject. Many of the great artists are supposed to have painted some really fine pictures in that style. In fact, there is quite a history of it."

"I've seen one or two books like that," she admitted.

"Well, I have a few special photos taken in Japan. They're really not so bad—more interesting than anything. Do you want to see them?"

"Certainly," she said, not actually sure that she did. She knew the subject had made its own precarious niche in art and literature. As a matter of fact, one of the books she had read had been well written and had kindled a hot excitement in her.

"Then I'll show them to you," Miles decided. "Just remember that I collected them as part of my interest in photography."

He went to his closet and brought down a thick envelope from a shelf and removed the pictures.

"These are really interesting," he said.

She took the pictures and felt a blush come again as she viewed the first one. But with the blush there was also a quick stir of aroused feeling. Actually the picture had not been posed without a certain flair for art, she thought, and there was a semblance of good lighting and shadows.

She sat on the bed to look at them and he sat beside her. After a few moments his arm went about her and she felt the warmness of a hand over one breast. A disturbing restlessness such as she had never experienced before slid like quicksilver through her veins.

"They certainly leave nothing to the imagination," she observed.

"I guess men and women are only human everywhere," he replied, smiling strangely. He pushed her back on the bed and kissed her hard and urgently. His fingers sought the zipper of her housecoat, but she stopped him.

"Later," she whispered. "Let me see the rest of the pictures."

"They don't shock you?"

"We've done the same things, haven't we?" she laughed softly.

He got got up, saying, "Wait, I'll show you another." He went to the closet and returned with an enlargement.

"Here's one."

She looked at it and abruptly she felt a shock of realization that made her gasp.

"Miles!"

"That's right. It's us. I fixed the Leica one night."

"No! Miles … you've got to—"

His fingers had found the zipper and jerked at it. In a quick panic of confusion she fought against him and tried to pull away, but he forced her back, his fingers hurting her shoulders. Then he grasped both of her wrists in one hand and held her arms above her head as he stripped the housecoat from her.

"Stop … please stop, Miles!" His intensity and roughness frightened her. She fought with greater effort but she was helpless against his tremendous strength.

When he had finished with her Thelma could not move. She knew that he rose and left her and put the pictures away and returned. After a moment she opened her eyes and found him standing over her, oddly smiling.

"You liked it that way," he murmured. "I could tell."

She fought to hold back tears and slowly got up from the bed and put on the housecoat. He waited until she had zipped it closed and then pulled her to him roughly and kissed her hard on her bruised mouth.

"We'd better get to bed now," he said. "We'll go for a long ride tomorrow."

She turned away from him, finding the door through her tears, and fled to her room. She closed the door and locked it, then flung herself on her bed, sobbing uncontrollably in the darkness of the room.

After a time she was silent, her thoughts a confusion of shame and disgust with herself. She heard Miles turn on his TV in his room, the click the switch made, and knew that he was using his earphones.

He couldn't hear her if she went to the bathroom now. She got up and unlocked the door. She moved quickly to the bathroom and locked herself in. It was late to draw bath water, but she had to do it. She had to cleanse herself of as much of it as she could, even if the bath water was partly symbolic.

When she returned to her room she locked the door and put on clean pajamas—although she usually slept in short nightgowns—obeying a deep compulsion to cover herself as much as possible; to protect herself and be as sterile of feminine allure as she could make herself.

Sleep was now a long ways off, she knew. With the cleansing of the bath had come a calmness. Deliberately she thought of the pictures he had taken of her in the nude, and then the one he had taken in the secrecy of their love-making.

She had to retrieve those pictures, especially the negatives. If she got the negatives and destroyed them he could never print more. No ... she would have to get the prints in his room, too. Then he couldn't make copies. And maybe she could get the negatives. They might be in the basement darkroom. No one ever went in there except Miles and herself, and Miles left the negatives in a filing box high on a shelf.

She would wait until she knew that he was asleep. She could hear him when he went to bed, the slight movement of his bed against the wall between them.

She knew all these small sounds, as she knew that the seldom used dining room was under his bedroom and that there was little likelihood of sounds from his room being heard below. Also, she knew that her room was against one wall of his room, and that a storage closet was against his other wall so that there was no one to hear when she was with him. Furthermore, there was little activity in the house after nine o'clock at night. Each of these things was important in protecting the secret of her affair with Miles.

So she would wait until she heard the sound of his getting into bed and after a while she would creep out and go down to the basement to search for the negatives.

She had not known Miles as he was tonight. The strange light in his eyes, the cruel strength of his fingers, the ruthlessness of his possession of her had frightened her profoundly. Their wild, fierce love-making had been entirely different from what it had been before—so different from the way it had been with Dan. She wished she could see Dan now; that he had never gone to Alaska.

Her shoulders ached and she knew that her soft white flesh would show the ugly discoloration of bruises. Her mouth felt crushed and her lips were swollen and sore. She lay very still and listened. Occasionally a car passed outside and she sensed that it was growing very late. Miles probably was watching the late movie.

She heard a car enter the driveway across the street and a car door slam and then the dull drone of men's voices. A house door opened and closed. After a while the door opened again and there were muffled voices; the sound of a car door opening and closing; a car starting and driving away down the street.

Then Thelma heard movement in Miles' room and finally the protesting squeak of springs as he got into bed. She waited ten minutes, then got up and tip-toed into the hallway. She carried a flashlight with her and quickly descended the stairs to the basement and darkroom.

She had to stand on an empty apple box to reach the negative file on the high shelf. She opened it and saw that there were a great many, each filed in a small envelope.

She took the file to the work bench in the darkroom and turned on the light in the viewing box that Miles had built. She opened the first envelope and began her search.

This was a negative of a girl in the nude, but it was not of her. She was about to discard it when she looked more closely. There was no doubt. The girl's hands were tied with a short piece of white rope and the girl stood against a background of heavy underbrush that was lighted as a picture is lighted when taken at night with a flash bulb.

Nausea attacked her and she swallowed hard. Then she knew sudden fright as she had never known it before.

She had to get to the police. Now! Just as she was. She didn't dare go back upstairs nor make a sound that might awaken Miles. She couldn't even risk using the telephone in the downstairs hallway.

The people across the street probably were still up. She would go there in her pajamas and explain and they could call the police. Even if the police saw the pictures of her it didn't matter. Or, maybe she could get them first somehow when they came.

She snapped off the viewer and picked up her flashlight and turned toward the door that she had carefully closed. Even as she reached for the nob, the door slowly opened and Miles stood there with a flashlight in his own hand.

He reached forward and wrenched her light from her, then swung the beam of his to the table and the small disorder of negatives and envelopes. He grasped her with one hand and quickly turned on the viewer and put a negative before it. He snapped off the viewer in a quick, hard flip and whirled her around so that she was pressed back against him and a hand covered her mouth.

"So you found out," he said very quietly.

Thelma tried to get away, but the flashlight beam made a downward flash and she felt her knees buckle as Miles' flashlight jarred across the side of her face.

"You shouldn't have looked, Thelma."

He pushed her toward the door and closed it before he snapped on the overhead light.

In the fullness of the overhead light she briefly saw the wideness of his eyes and the depth of panic in them. He was being too deliberate. His voice was too toneless. She remembered that he had murdered …

"I'll have to come back," he said. "I haven't time now." He seemed to be talking to himself. "I'll come back and do it right so that they won't find her too soon. Then I'll have time. After the other. I'll have to take her somewhere else. In her car. That's the way. In her car and leave her somewhere."

In a frantic burst of strength she tried to free herself, but his strength was immense. With his free hand he ripped the pajama tops from her and fashioned a gag. He forced her to the floor and held her with one knee and his full weight as he jerked an extension cord free and used it to bind her. Then he left her on the floor, snapped off the light and closed the door after him as he left.

He walked quietly across the basement, then Thelma heard the creak of stairs as he went up and knew that he was using the outside entrance to the basement.

Afterward it was very quiet and dark. The coldness of the cement floor pressed against the bareness of her breasts where he had left her face down. She managed to turn onto her back and stare into the blackness.

"He's going to kill me," she thought while a horrible, chilling fear clutched at her heart. "He's the man they're trying to find and he's going to kill me …"

CHAPTER SEVENTEEN
MARY JO CAMMAN

After Cal Horlick left, Mary Jo washed the coffee cups and made sandwiches for Bill. The small kitchen tasks failed to relieve the restless tension that Cal's visit had left in her. She remembered the things that had been said, but more poignantly the things that had not been said and the truths she had learned about herself.

Hearing a car stop in front, she glanced out the window. A police car was parked squarely in front of the house and she saw the outlines of two men in it. The precaution was unnecessary, she thought. Or was it? Was she really in danger?

Whatever the answer might be to that, she had nothing to say about it. Suddenly, because a man had raped her, a great many people were concerned about her safety. Her husband had changed. Cal Horlick had all but taken her in her own bed. It was almost as if she had become a coveted prize in the eyes of all men.

The quick memory of the moment upstairs disturbed her. She realized that she had virtually promised to see him again in circumstances that could well be the same. Possibly he would ask her to his apartment, and she was not certain that she would not go.

"Maybe that would end it," she thought. "Maybe I could once and for all rid myself of whatever has come over me. Maybe now I need to deliberately have another man to complete the cycle and bring it back to normalcy with Bill. Only that wouldn't do it for Bill. Just for me. And possibly not for me. But it would be easy with Cal."

She shook her head impatiently, abruptly unhappy with her thoughts. She didn't want to be this way, nor to think this way. She wished desperately that everything could be as it was before that night.

She went into the living room and turned on the television set. A late movie was just starting and she settled down to watch it, forcing her attention to the screen.

By the time Bill called she had become engrossed in the picture and had achieved a measure of calmness. His familiar voice brought her further reassurance.

He was curious about Cal's visit, but if she read any suspicion into his voice she told herself it was because she nursed a small feeling of guilt about what had happened upstairs and the trend of her conversation with Cal.

"I've got to stop this!" she scolded herself and returned to the television. It kept her occupied until Bill came home and she heard the familiar sound of their car driving up the driveway to the garage.

He invited the two policemen in for coffee and sandwiches. They were young, well-built, and very polite. They made her very conscious of a false concept she had subconsciously always held about the police. These men did not fit the rough, tough, hard role of the policeman she usually visualized. They were clean-cut, intelligent, and smoothly at ease.

After they left, she sat at the table with Bill and they finished the coffee.

"What was all that business about the window?" he asked.

She told him about Horlick's interest in the window across the street and sighting the visibility across the bed.

"I never noticed a window over there," Bill said. "Did you?"

"Not until a few nights ago when Carrie and I were up there. She noticed it. There was some odd flashing of light behind the blind."

"I'll take a look when we go up," he said and stretched. "Saturday nights drag down there. Ready for bed?"

She nodded and picked up the cups and saucers and left them in the sink. She could wash them in the morning. Bill waited until she had gone up, then checked the doors and turned off the downstairs lights. He unplugged the telephone to take it to the bedroom where an auxiliary plug was behind their bedside table.

When he went up she already was in her nightgown and was washing her face in the bathroom. He waited in the bedroom for her, idly undressing and putting on pajamas. Occasionally he glanced at the window.

When she came in he was standing at the window looking out into the night.

"That's the window over there?" he asked, pointing.

Mary Jo stood beside him and looked out. "The blind is up now. That's the one. When the trees had more leaves on them I didn't notice that you could see in here from that point."

"What does Horlick think?"

"He said that the man seemed to know our movements, and that he evidently knew I was up here that night."

"It's a point," Bill admitted. "I hope they'll check it."

"They're going to tomorrow."

They turned from the window and went to their beds. "Guess I should have pulled the blind," Bill grinned.

She smiled and said, "I hardly think anyone's up this late." She saw him look at her with the stirring of desire and realized that she welcomed it. "Do you want to?" she asked simply.

"Yes. Do you?"

"I'll get ready …" She started to get up, but saw the way he was staring past her at the window. "What's wrong, Bill?"

"I'm certain I saw a movement in that window over there. It looked like a reflection of light on glass. A car just passed and I saw the flash."

"Probably from the windowpane."

"No. It was different." He walked to the bedroom window and looked intently at the other house. "Two separate reflections. Binoculars, I think."

He turned abruptly and picked up the telephone from the bed table. "I'm going to call the police."

She reached out and caught his hand. Suddenly it made no difference to her if someone was at the other window or not. She was tired of these invasions of her privacy. She could pull down the blind, and that would be that. She had to find out now … with Bill. They could be so near a return to normalcy, and an answer to the questions that so deeply disturbed her.

"Don't call now, Bill. There'll be time in the morning."

"But they might catch him now! If there's someone there."

"He'd see a police car come. No, wait until morning. I'll pull the blind."

Reluctantly he released the telephone, staring at the window across the street. Mary Jo got up and pulled down the blind and turned to Bill.

"There! Let's not let anything spoil it for us tonight, Bill. Please?"

He looked at her and smiled slowly. "That's the best idea I've heard in a month of Sundays, darling!" He stood and took her close in his arms, their shadows falling upon the drawn blind.

"I think so," she said.

If she could only recapture the easiness and camaraderie they once had known! She would try in every way she knew. Then, perhaps, the doubts would leave her.

"Wait," she said. "I'll be right back, Mister."

"Don't worry, ma'am … I'm not going anywhere!"

Bill had turned out the overhead light and only the softer glow of the bedside lamp filled the room when Mary Jo returned. He was on the bed, waiting for her, and his eyes moved slowly and appreciatively up and down her body which was clearly outlined beneath the thin sheath of her nightgown.

Mary Jo approached the bed and smiled down at him. A heavy pulse was hammering inside her and there was a quickening surge of feeling in her breasts.

"It won't be much fun with a nightgown on," she murmured.

He grinned. "You could take it off."

"You do it," she said softly.

Despite the leanness of his body, there was a firm sheath of muscles under his skin and Mary Jo felt a thrill of anticipation slide along her nerves as she watched the sinewy play of his muscles when he rose from the bed and came to her.

He lifted the nightgown over her head and tossed it to a chair. Then he held her against him, all the curves and hollows of her body blending with his, and kissed her hungrily. Then all the magic of her love for him flowed out in her sudden sweet surrender …

Later, she stared into the darkness of the room as she listened to his even breathing and knew that he had fallen almost immediately into sleep.

A dull ache of frustration held her and brought a shadow of moisture to her eyes. She had tried hard. She had made it good for him until he had cried out in his own rapture. Yet he seemed almost like a stranger ... almost as if he had bought and paid for her. And she had failed to find the elusive, tantalizing ecstasy she sought. It had been almost static for her, and she knew that her feeble pretense of enjoyment had had no basis in fact.

Remembering the night the stranger had come, she recalled with a mixed sense of shame, outrage and furtive pleasure, how recklessly her latent passions had risen to confound her. Then her mind had wandered and the image of the rapist became confused with that of Cal Horlick until she had recklessly abandoned herself to the fantasy that it was he who possessed her in mounting intensity. After a moment, the sound of Bill's voice had shattered the fantasy and she had clung to her husband and the pretense had begun and was carried through to conclusion.

Now her reflections tumbled in a repetitive confusion as she sought an elusive answer.

And finally she forced it from her mind and willed her consciousness into a red-black curtain before her closed eyes. After a time she felt sleep closing in upon her and she relaxed and welcomed it with relief.

CHAPTER EIGHTEEN
MILES SALIN

After Thelma had left him, still disturbed about the pictures she had seen, Miles sat quietly in a chair. For the moment the demanding compulsions that drove him had subsided in the temporary satiation afforded by Thelma. In moments like these, he was afraid. The enormity of his crimes came sharply into focus and he was fearful of the consequences.

The fact that he had added murder to his violations of women was his greatest fear. For this crime he could be put to death. At the penitentiary there was a small, one-room house that was a gas chamber.

He could be led into that one room and strapped in a chair. Small pellets would be dropped into a liquid and the lethal gas fumes would rise and surround him and come to his nostrils and destroy him.

If only the man had not struggled. He remembered the confusion of grappling in the dark, the pitting of strength against one another, and the flash of realization that the gun was against the other man's head. Pulling the trigger had been almost completely automatic.

For this small reflex of mind and muscles they could kill him now if they caught him. For the rest of his life he would be running, evasive, cautious; living in fear of a hand descending upon his shoulder, and the voice of a cop in his ear.

No one would suspect him, though. He would be careful to never let it happen again. There was no need to let it happen again. Now he had Thelma, and this was a better way. There could be others later on.

He turned on the television set and adjusted the headset to his ears. Sometimes when he was frightened by the murder and the things he had done, television made him forget the fright.

It was a very long show and it was late when it ended. He turned off the set and, remembering that it was Saturday night, he raised the window blind and looked at the house across the street. Lights were on downstairs.

His room was dark after turning off the television set, and for several moments he was a tall, dark outline in his window against the outside light of night.

Before long the couple across the street would go upstairs to the bedroom. In preparation he brought the binoculars from a dresser drawer. Then, as he waited, he stretched out on the bed. He could see the glow when the bedroom light in the other house was turned on.

It was only a few moments, and he returned to the window and watched. He saw Mary Jo Camman come into the bedroom and turn on the light. She undressed quickly while he watched through the glasses. He saw her put on a nightgown and go out of the room and a few moments later Bill Camman entered his range of vision. He plugged a telephone into a line and put the instrument on a bedtable, and then he leisurely undressed and got into pajamas.

He buttoned the front of the pajamas, stretched, massaged his head vigorously for a moment and walked to the window and looked out. He still was standing there, outlined against the light behind him, when Miles caught a glimpse of Mary Jo coming into the room. She spoke and her husband turned. She looked puzzled by what he evidently said, and then he reached suddenly toward the telephone, with a slight, tense backward movement of his head as if he was speaking about something he had seen outside.

Miles saw the mild protest in her face and the way she stopped the reaching hand. Her husband reluctantly replaced the telephone without dialing and stared through the window, straight at Miles.

Mary Jo went to the window and pulled down the blind. Miles watched her silhouette as she turned. Then her husband was standing there and they embraced.

A cold chill of fear held Miles as he watched the small tableau. He knew for a certainty that he had been discovered. Obviously Camman had been on the point of calling the police and his wife had stopped him. She wanted to make love.

All of this had been silently acted out for him. Tomorrow they would call the police and there would be questions. Not only would they question him, but they would question Thelma, and now he was not certain of what Thelma would do. She might say something about the pictures.

Even as he stood motionless, feeling the first evidence of panic, he heard her door open and close stealthily and her soft footsteps in the hallway. He listened for the sound of the bathroom door opening and closing, but the sound did not come. Abruptly he realized that she must have gone downstairs.

The pictures! She wanted the negatives of the pictures he had taken of her, and if she searched in the darkroom she would find other negatives. She would know for a certainty who he was.

He was on the verge of being discovered within a few moments. The couple in the old house would call the police in the morning and report their suspicions about the window. But immediately—right now—Thelma might have found the negatives of pictures he had taken out in the woods. He should never have left those negatives in the darkroom, but he and Thelma were the only ones who ever entered it. The hiding place on the top shelf had seemed even safer than his room. Except that Thelma knew about it.

He had to stop them. All of them! Even if only long enough for him to get out of town.

If he had the gun he would have a weapon to assure him complete control over the three persons. But the gun was at the parking lot.

Hurriedly Miles opened a drawer and brought out the makeshift blackjack he had fashioned weeks before. He slipped it into a hip pocket of his blues. He would go to the basement and if Thelma was there he would have to silence her. He had to plan what he would do, but before he could make any arrangements for getting away, he had to stop Thelma from going to the police if she had discovered the secret. She might do that immediately.

Then he must stop the couple across the street from calling. He must have time to get away and put as many miles as possible between him and the city and the small room with the gas.

Quietly he left the room and started down the stairs …

After Miles left Thelma in the darkroom, he returned upstairs to his room and put on his coveralls. He put the ropes and tape in his pockets; the blackjack and the hood. He didn't suppose it would make much difference if they saw him to recognize him or not. They wouldn't live to tell anyone who he was. But this was almost like a uniform for work, now. This was the different person he could be. The different person was the one who could do the things that had to be done. First across the street. Then he would return for Thelma and take her out in the woods.

He was glad that he had not killed her in the basement. He could make her walk to the car. This was better. And leaving her in the woods would make it more difficult for anyone to find her.

He left the house and crossed the street. In the darkness of the back yard he put on the hood and went to the back door. It was locked.

He remembered reading in a mystery story how to do this, and he had the tape, and the blackjack would be just right. He unrolled a generous length of tape and tore it free from the roll. He pressed the tape firmly against one of the small panes of window in the back door. One end of the tape he held in his left hand as he firmly knocked out the section of window with a single sharp rap. The tape held the glass from falling. There was only the sound of the single crack of the blackjack against the glass. He reached in and unlocked the door.

They didn't hear him in the bedroom. He knew why they probably slept so soundly. He stood quietly in the doorway listening. He heard a long sigh and there was movement. He walked to a bed.

"Are you up, Bill?" Mary Jo's voice sounded sleepy.

"Huh?" Her husband's voice was thick with sudden awakening. "What did you … ?"

He saw Miles coming toward him then and threw up an arm to defend himself. Miles hit the arm with the blackjack and Mary Jo screamed. Miles hit Camman again and whirled to lean over Mary Jo. He slapped her hard and she stopped screaming.

Camman was motionless and moaning. Miles looked back at Mary Jo and by the dim light from the window he saw the terror in her face.

"I don't want to hurt you," he said dully. Something had gone wrong deep inside him. She was too pretty. Even when she was frightened like this. She looked too soft and warm and desirable.

He didn't want to bring blood to her face and batter it and hurt her.

He lifted the hood and held her firmly by the chin and gently kissed her.

"Poor baby," he whispered. "Poor baby. You were so good. I don't want to hurt you. I don't want to kill you."

Soundlessly she moved in a violent effort to free herself. He fell over her to pin her down, and now he was laughing. "That's better, baby! Fight me, you bitch! I can do it then!"

Fingernails raked across his face and the pain sent wild, singing delight through him. Now he could do it! This was like the night he had killed the man.

He rolled on the bed to pinion her between his legs and he felt the man come from the other bed and claw at his arms. It didn't matter now. Mary Jo was clinging desperately to one of his arms. He concentrated on tearing it away from her grasp to bring it up and chop down hard with the blackjack.

A movement at his side flickered across the corner of his vision and he turned his head. Camman was on his feet and swinging down hard with something in his hand.

For just an instant Miles saw what it was, and then the telephone crashed against the side of his head over his temple and he dropped in a dead weight across Mary Jo.

He was dazed for only seconds. Camman continued to swing the telephone against his head. Mary Jo had managed to get away from him and was on the floor.

Miles fell off the bed on top of her, away from Camman. Somehow he got to his feet and stumbled toward the door.

Neither of them followed him.

CHAPTER NINETEEN
LIEUTENANT MARTIN

"Anything more, Salin?" Martin asked.

Miles shook his head. "That's all, Lieutenant."

"Did you intend to kill the Cammans?"

"I guess so. I don't know. I was frightened. The way he looked at my window and then reached for the phone."

"You guessed right. Only he should have called us then."

"What happens next, Lieutenant?"

"You're entitled to a lawyer. Do you know one?"

"No. I haven't any money. Doesn't the court appoint one, or something like that?"

"Yes."

"Camman? Did I hurt him much?"

"Bruised arm and a slight concussion. He'll be all right."

"I'm glad about that. I feel sorry for him. I know the Cammans pretty well. I mean, watching them like I told you. I think she's always been a little disappointed in him. He isn't much of a man."

"Enough to put you on the run."

"I don't mean that."

"Okay. Anything more you want to say?" Martin asked. He was tired and he had been awakened at half past three. The case was finished except for routine. The rest was up to Horlick.

"Why did I do all those things?"

"You'll have to ask a psychiatrist, Salin. I don't know the answers." He looked at Duffey who stood near a window listening. Duffey shrugged and lit a cigarette. The shrug was a silent confirmation of Martin's thought. You never knew how these guys would act, what they thought, or what made them the way they were.

"I never really hurt any of those women," Salin said.

A police stenographer raised a questioning look at Martin. The detective nodded at him. "We don't need this stuff," he said. "You've got the confession. Get it typed. Horlick will be here any time. He'll want to see it."

The stenographer got up and left the office. Martin stared at Salin thoughtfully.

"What did you intend to do with those pictures?" he asked.

"Just look at them, I guess."

"You didn't take any of Mrs. Camman?"

Miles shook his head. "I hadn't thought of the pictures then. She was the first one. The pictures came later."

"One more thing, Salin. Before you attacked Mrs. Camman, you pulled down the blind, didn't you?"

Salin nodded.

"Why?" Martin asked.

"I didn't want anyone looking in."

"But the only place you could see their window was from yours, wasn't it? I mean, see it well enough to look in."

"Yes. I didn't think of that. I guess I was afraid that Thelma might go into my room or something. She could have seen. I don't know why I did it. I just did."

Martin looked at Duffey. "That's the thing that was bothering me. Remember? I told you something was gnawing at me. But I couldn't tab it. Makes sense now, though. I should have tagged it then. Only one person would know you could see into that bedroom with those trees blocking off the view. The person standing in Salin's window. And only that person would instinctively pull down the blind. I should have caught it."

"I don't know if I'll buy that, George," Duffey said. "Maybe any guy about to rape a woman would pull down a blind."

Martin rubbed his jaw and finally nodded. "So maybe it wasn't such a good idea, after all. Okay, Duffey. We may as well put him away until Horlick gets here."

Duffey came over to Salin and took him by the arm and the two men left the office. Martin sat at his desk and stared at the chair just vacated by Salin. Now the heat would be off and Horlick would be busy making headlines.

The capture had been unspectacular and quick. Salin had run across the street and up to his room for the keys to the Jorgson woman's garage and car. Camman had called in and a prowl car got there in time to pick up Salin just as he backed out of the garage.

The landlady had identified him and suggested that Thelma Jorgson, who lived in the room next to his, might have more information. Thelma had not answered the knock at her door and one of the men downstairs heard thumping in the basement. They found her in the darkroom. It didn't take long to get the full story and Salin confessed.

The telephone on Martin's desk rang and he answered. It was his wife.

"Are you coming back for breakfast, George?"

"No. I'll eat downtown. It's that rapist case. We got him."

"Oh, I'm glad! You're all right?"

"Sure. They had him here on ice by the time I got down. But Horlick's due and there'll be a lot doing."

He hung up and was about to leave his desk when the door opened and Cal Horlick came in. The assistant district attorney looked grim.

"They tell me you got a full confession," he said. "What are the details?"

Martin rapidly reviewed them. Horlick listened and nodded occasionally.

"You should get an easy conviction," Martin concluded.

"I will," Horlick said with satisfaction.

And headlines, Martin thought. He watched Horlick open the door and go out. Now the pressure was off. Getting Salin had been luck, and because a thin, tired-looking newspaperman had the guts to swing a telephone. But that made no difference in the end result. The murderer and rapist was behind bars and the public would be satisfied, Horlick would be satisfied, and there would be no criticism heaped upon the department.

He still had the file on the case in front of him on the desk. He looked through the pictures they had brought in from the man's room—at the small negatives and a few contact prints they'd found in the darkroom.

He selected an enlargement and frowned. Beside it he placed several others. They actually had little bearing on the case, he thought. He picked up his telephone and talked to a desk man.

"Is the Jorgson woman still out there? Good. Send her in."

A few moments later Thelma Jorgson came into the office. She looked tired and distraught. She took the chair Martin indicated and sat down with a small sigh of weariness.

"There are some pictures of you here," he said. "I think you know what they are."

She blushed and nodded.

"I don't believe they have any particular importance in the case. The others that tie him in with the rape cases and the murder are the important ones. I'm going to ask the D.A.'s office to keep these out of sight unless it's absolutely necessary to show them."

"Thank you, Lieutenant," she murmured. Her eyes expressed a gratefulness that embarrassed him.

"I just wanted to let you know," he said. "So you won't mention them to anyone. Understand? Especially to any newspapermen."

"I understand."

He looked at her silently for a moment. "Are you going to be all right about this?" he asked.

"I think so. I wasn't in love with him. Not really."

"Okay. You can go home. Don't leave town, though. Not without notifying us."

He stood and went to the door with her. In a few moments he would go into the Chief's office and give his report.

Duffey joined him for the short walk down a hallway to the chief's door. "Need me?" he asked Martin.

"No. It's okay."

"Yeah. This ends it."

Martin glanced at him and shook his head a trifle. "Not entirely. It's pretty well finished for us, but not for the people involved. Every one of those girls and women will remember from now on. The men. The family of the man who was murdered. Any relatives that Salin has. But mostly the women, Duffy."

"Like that Camman woman?"

"Like the Camman woman."

CHAPTER TWENTY
CAL HORLICK

The athletic club masseur was adept as he worked. He had strong fingers that found muscles and tendons with a certainty of touch and purpose. Cal Horlick relaxed and planned his afternoon's work.

His noonday workouts at the club twice a week paid off in a good many ways other than his physical trimness. He met men that he needed to know at the club; he achieved a certain popularity among them; and he found that he could think clearly and incisively when he was relaxing after a hard workout.

At the moment his mind was on the Salin case. It was coming to trial within the week and he was looking forward to the task outlined for him. There would be headlines from this one; a chance to work well in a courtroom; TV news coverage; the things that would help his career.

Point by point he reviewed the preparations that he had made for the prosecution, glad that the assignment was his. As he went over the witnesses in his mind, he remembered the telephone call from Bill Camman that morning.

Camman's office wanted Bill to go to the southern part of the state for two days to cover a story. He had asked if it was all right, and Horlick assured him that there would be no need for him until the trial started.

Now Cal suddenly realized that Mary Jo would be alone in town, and he remembered their conversation. He stirred a little under the masseur's hands.

"Better call it a day, Joe," he said over his shoulder. "I've got to get back to work."

He dressed hurriedly and looked up the insurance firm's telephone number in a pay booth and placed a call to Mary Jo. She recognized his voice at once.

Cal explained, "Bill asked if it would be all right for him to leave town. Said he was leaving this afternoon ... so that leaves you free for dinner with me. If you will ..."

She hesitated briefly and then said, "Official business, Cal?"

"I'll be honest. Personal," he admitted. "Perfectly safe, though," he added with a chuckle.

"I'm not sure if it would be wise for us to be seen," she said. "You're awfully well known around town."

"We could broil steaks at my apartment. There's a private entrance ... if that bothers you."

"That sounds even more dangerous, Cal."

"Let's not be clandestine about it," he laughed. "I'll take you to the busiest place in town, a place out in the country, or home. But we didn't finish a talk. Remember?"

"I remember."

"Do you want to finish it?"

"I think I do, Cal."

"Over dinner?"

"Yes, over dinner. Is your apartment all right? Really, I mean? I don't want any talk about us."

"It's safe. Shall I pick you up after work?"

"All right," she said. She named a street corner and a time and Cal hung up. Thoughtfully he left the booth and went to a parking lot for his car. He was glad that he was possibly on the verge of settling this thing between Mary Jo and himself.

They had finished the steaks and coffee and Mary Jo had insisted upon doing the dishes. Now they sat in the sprawling living room of his apartment. The lights were muted and low music came from a high fidelity speaker enclosure.

"I've never done anything like this before," Mary Jo said, smiling as if she were amused with herself.

"Times change, Mary Jo," he grinned. "There was a time when bachelors didn't entertain without seduction in mind. At least, the world assumed that."

"Have times really changed so much?" she asked piquantly.

"Maybe not. If I thought I could, I probably would be tempted to try."

"Now we're trying to make light, gay and leading conversation," she said. "You said you wanted to talk with me. Seriously, I hope."

He nodded. "I don't know where to start because I don't know exactly what I want."

"You want me, don't you?"

"That's a nice, blunt answer that neatly sums up the case."

"Then what's your problem?"

"If you weren't married, I think I'd ask you to marry me."

"But I'm married. I intend to stay married, Cal. Does that answer some of it for you?"

"Obviously."

She leaned toward a coffee table and took a cigarette and lit it, looking over the top of the match at him.

"No, Cal. Not obviously," she said. "There are all sorts of relationships between men and women. For instance, you might think of asking me to be your mistress. You'd just think about it, I believe. You wouldn't ask."

"If I didn't know you so well—"

"You don't know me well, Cal. I don't know myself any more. I'm not trying to shock you, nor paint a picture of me that isn't a true picture. Nor would I have talked like this a few months ago. I think I've explained this once before … about myself."

"That night."

"Maybe I'm curious about myself. Maybe I think that I have to really know about myself."

He took a long, slow breath and looked at her squarely, thinking that she was a lovely woman—a mature, complete woman with an inherent vitality and sex appeal that should stir any man's blood.

"All right," he said. "If we're going to be this way, I'll slice through some more red tape. Will you go to bed with me?"

She regarded him thoughtfully, as if she were turning his words over in contemplative inspection, to learn if she was angry with his suggestion, or pleased, or afraid of it.

"This is the strange part," she finally said. "The part I don't understand. A few months ago I would have been repulsed by the idea, and the thought of being unfaithful to Bill would have been something shameful. But now I can think about it and actually wonder if I do want to go to bed with you."

"It's not just because you're a desirable woman that I want you," he said. "Let's make that clear. That summer at the beach—"

"I know that, too, or otherwise I might be angry. Don't you think I felt something, too, that summer?" Her features were alive and there was a warm glow in her eyes. "You could have had me. As a matter of fact, you started to have me."

Cal smiled, feeling again the embarrassment, but not bothered by it now as he once had been. Maturity and experience changed things. But all of this was inconsistent with Mary Jo as he had known her, nor did he believe that he was so attractive to her. He shook his head and said, "This is all talk. You wouldn't cheat, and it would be cheating in your book. I'm not sure that I'd like it, either. I like Bill."

Mary Jo thought about it with the same contemplative expression that she had worn before, and again she spoke evenly and almost judiciously.

"I think if I'd did, it would be for Bill's sake. I don't expect you to understand that. Something happened to me—against my will—but nevertheless it happened. Since then it hasn't been right. Not as it should be. Maybe I can regain it. Maybe it would be better for Bill ... for Bill and me."

Her meaning was confused to him, but he had a glimmer of understanding that left him with mixed emotions.

"You're talking about the rape. Is that it?"

"Of course."

"That something happened then?"

She looked at him without answering. He studied her face for seconds and then said, "Tell me something, Mary Jo ... can a woman enjoy rape? Is that it?"

She looked away, her eyes suddenly veiled and he got to his feet and stood near her. Bending down, he took her chin in his hand and forced her to meet his glance.

"I'm not very smart about some things," he said softly. "I've never been married. But it occurs to me that perhaps you got something out of rape that you never had from Bill. And now you have to find out whether it was the circumstances of rape that did it ... or if Bill has failed."

"You're very frank."

A quick, resentful anger came to him for an instant. "I'm not a stud, Mary Jo," he said.

She jerked away from his hand and sprang up. Her hand was a stinging slash across his face. Instinctively he gripped her arms and held her motionless and glared down at her.

Anger brought a highlight of color to her cheeks, and her eyes were bright and clear. Beneath his hands he felt the firmness of her arms, and she was so close to him that he was conscious of her body heat, the full and voluptuous lines of her figure.

"But I will be, if that's what you want," he snapped. The impulse was sudden and natural. He held her brutally close, grinding his mouth against hers, forcing the soft lips open, immobilizing her desperate efforts to break away. After a moment she was quiet and he released her.

"The bedroom is in there," he nodded.

"I'm sorry. I had that coming," she said softly. She put a hand on his arm. "What else could you think?"

She spoke in a flat, matter-of-fact voice without anger and almost in self-chastisement.

He was startled to realize that now he wanted her, when he had only felt a frustrated anger and desire to punish her a few moments before. He had a vague feeling that she had been waiting for him to take the initiative; that her coming to his apartment was in itself a commitment—a testament of her intentions toward him.

If he had blundered upon the reason for her behavior, he knew that the question was still great and demanding in her mind—and in her body.

Beyond the contemplated act he refused to think of consequences. He knew that they stood there in the face of all the risks that could challenge his political career and his personal ambitions.

An emotional liaison could mean political death—if it were exposed to the public. And marriage was not to be thought of with Mary Jo. At least, not without weeks, months, even years of building and adjustment. She had convinced him of that.

In the immediate moment there was only the opportunity to force this thing between them into a primitive solution, once and for all.

"We'll find out," Cal said simply and took her hungrily in his arms again. Their mouths fused hotly and Mary Jo was immediately aware of the powerful urgency of his passion. She returned his kiss with an ardor that matched his own but then, strangely, the tumult drained out of her and her lips grew stiff and unresponsive under his.

Cal sensed her withdrawal, yet he did not release her until she pushed against his chest with her hands. He drew back, then, and regarded her with a narrowed concentration while his aroused breathing soughed gustily from his lungs.

He saw that Mary Jo's face was troubled and anxious and there was a faint film of tears in her eyes.

"I'm sorry, Cal," she murmured contritely, "I can't go ahead with it. Even if it were good between us, I'd never be able to keep my marriage alive. In many ways it's a good marriage and I've betrayed Bill by even coming here."

"Mary Jo, I've a feeling we're going to miss the greatest experience of our lives." Cal's voice was tight with emotion.

She laughed softly. "Don't be angry, Cal. It's just that I've suddenly realized that my husband is the nicest person in my life. Can you understand that?"

He nodded sadly. "Do you mind my telling you that you're wonderful?"

"It's a lovely compliment, Cal. And you mustn't disparage yourself. Truly. It's just something else—something warm and good that comes to a man and woman who have shared things together in the intimacy of marriage."

The very friendliness of her voice gave him a warm, good feeling. Abruptly Cal liked her better than ever before.

"Okay, we'll forget it, then," he said.

"It's better that we do."

She ran her fingers through her hair and straightened her dress. "Will you take me home now?"

"If that's what you want ..." He kissed her lightly and guided her to the door.

CHAPTER TWENTY-ONE
THELMA JORGSON

On the night that she moved from Mrs. Lindicott's place, Thelma walked across the street to the Camman house and rang the doorbell. Mary Jo came to the door dressed in a house-dress and apron.

"Oh … Miss Jorgson," she smiled, a small expression of surprise in her eyes. "Won't you come in?"

"Just for a few moments," Thelma said, almost apologetically. Now that she was here, she wasn't certain why she had come, except that she had to talk with someone. And it had to be someone who *knew*. "If you were in the kitchen, we can talk there."

"I still have some coffee left," Mary Jo said, opening the door wide. "My husband went out of town yesterday, so I just had a pick-up dinner tonight and I'm late."

The large, old-fashioned kitchen gave Thelma a feeling of nostalgia for the farmhouse where she had been reared. It was homey and comfortable and she was glad that Mary Jo had accepted her suggestion. It would be easier to talk here.

Mary Jo poured coffee for them and they sat at the kitchen table. They tasted the steaming liquid, and Thelma's hostess looked at her with a question in her eyes.

Thelma smiled nervously and said, "I really just wanted to visit for a few moments. I'm moving tomorrow and I didn't know if I'd get another chance. And because of Miles …" She hesitated and knew that she was blushing. "Maybe you'd rather not talk about it."

"Are you moving because of what happened?"

"Mrs. Lindicott asked me to move. I don't have to tell you what they found in his room and downstairs. Mrs. Lindicott saw the pictures. I know you saw them because you were there after they brought him in from the garage to identify him. And the police had left the pictures on the table. I saw you look at them."

Mary Jo nodded. "Please don't worry about it, Miss Jorgson."

"Thelma … and may I call you Mary Jo?"

"Please do."

"I don't want you to think … that is, I'm not that kind of a woman. Miles just had a way, I guess. Actually I work in a doctor's office. I've never—"

Mary Jo smiled. "You don't have to explain, Thelma. I'm just thankful that you escaped. He's very dangerous."

Thelma lifted her coffee cup and then put it down without drinking.

"Do you think he'll be executed?" she asked bluntly.

"I don't know. Evidently his lawyer is going to try to prove that he is insane." Mary Jo shook her head. "Maybe he is. It doesn't seem possible that a sane man would do the things he did. But you were around him quite a bit. What do you think?"

Thelma bit her lower lip and said slowly, "I don't know. I suppose most people would think he is, but working in a doctor's office and all … well, quite a few men do a lot of odd things and they certainly aren't regarded as being insane. Doctor is a gynecologist, and from case histories and things I've heard … well, I just don't know."

"But he murdered, too."

"Yes, that's different. I think he was frightened. And I guess he was going to kill me. That last night was different."

"I think he was a madman that night," Mary Jo said. She shuddered and picked up her coffee and drank some. "I'm still frightened when I think about it."

"I know. I have nightmares. That and ... well, I might as well be frank. Those horrible pictures. I hope no one else will ever see them."

"I don't know why anyone else should, Thelma. It doesn't seem to me that they're very important to the case. Not the pictures of you."

"Lieutenant Martin said he was going to try and keep them out of sight. But Mrs. Lindicott saw them and you did. I hope you won't—"

Mary Jo reached across the table and put a hand on one of Thelma's. "Please don't worry about me, or my husband. And I don't believe you'll have to worry about the police who saw them, either."

"If the doctor found out—"

"The newspapers just said that you were suspicious of some negatives you happened to see down there. How could the doctor find out?"

"Do you think Mrs. Lindicott would tell him?"

"I doubt it."

"Honestly, Mary Jo, I feel terrible about coming to you with my troubles this way."

"Please don't. And think how those other girls and women must feel. They *know* pictures of them will be shown. They're evidence."

The thought was comforting in a strange way. Thelma hadn't considered the other women before.

"I suppose I'm just thinking of myself," she admitted.

"There's no reason why you shouldn't. But don't worry too much about it. You'll be on the stand, but I don't believe they'll pry too much into your relationship with him."

Thelma managed a smile. "I'm glad I came over. I just *had* to talk with someone."

"Of course. And I'm glad you came."

She felt better after her visit with Mary Jo, but she still wasn't certain about Mrs. Lindicott. The visit across the street made her realize that she could talk about it, though, and on the way back to the rooming house she decided to squarely face Mrs. Lindicott with it.

The woman was in her kitchen with the small table radio on. She was tall, heavy, and well into her fifties. She looked at Thelma coldly and said, "Well?"

"I want to talk with you, Mrs. Lindicott. I told you I'd move, but I don't want you to tell people about … about some of the things you know."

Mrs. Lindicott turned down the radio and looked at Thelma with narrowed eyes.

"To think that I let a woman like you in my house," she said bitterly. "Those filthy pictures. You have no right to associate with anyone who is decent. Why on earth a doctor let's you—" She stopped speaking and her eyes widened. "He doesn't know. Of course he doesn't know! A doctor would never tolerate such a thing."

Thelma felt as if the blood had been drained from her, and that she would certainly fall if she did not grasp something. Her hand sought the edge of the table.

"You wouldn't dare!" she whispered.

"Oh, wouldn't I? Wait and see, young woman."

"Please, Mrs. Lindicott … you can't do that!"

Mrs. Lindicott stood, several inches taller than Thelma, and glared down at the smaller woman.

"See that you're out of here in the morning," she snapped.

❧   ❧   ❧

Thelma fled from the kitchen and ran up the stairs to her room. She slammed the door and locked it. She should never have talked again with Mrs. Lindicott. She was not certain now that she should have talked with Mary Jo Camman.

If she had to leave the doctor she would be leaving most of her life. It had been too long now. The receptionist's office, her desk, her typewriter, Doctor. She never had realized how important they were to her.

Now in the morning he would get a call from Mrs. Lindicott. That outraged, prim, accusing voice would tell him about the pictures—and describe what his receptionist had been doing nights at the rooming house.

Suddenly Thelma realized what she had to do before Mrs. Lindicott talked with Doctor.

She finished her packing and went downstairs and called a taxi. She had paid for her room, so she wouldn't have to see Mrs. Lindicott again. Hurriedly she brought down her traveling bags and several shopping bags loaded with other belongings and waited at the door for the taxi.

The driver loaded them for her and looked at her questioningly. She named a hotel and within half an hour she was in a hotel room undressing for bed. She had placed an early call, and she hoped that she could sleep.

At six o'clock in the morning she called the desk and cancelled the call. She had not slept all night. She tried to erase the fatigue from her face with cold water and cosmetics and went downstairs and ate in the hotel coffee shop. She was at the office an hour early.

"Doctor, may I speak with you a moment?"

He looked up from his desk and smiled. "Certainly, Thelma. Trouble?" He wore his white coat and was ready to see patients— a middle-aged, efficient, soft-voiced man who was beginning to show gray in his hair, and had a slight bulge at his waistline.

Thelma nodded. "It's about this ... this mess I'm in."

"I thought it might be. Can I help?"

"You'll probably want me to leave," she said.

He closed the case history he had been studying and gave her his full attention. "I doubt that," he said. "But if you have a reason for saying that, you'd better give it to me. At least, it will clear your mind. Why don't you sit down?"

She took a chair and tried to think of a starting place. The doctor watched her and waited, looking very much as he did when he interviewed a patient. She felt a great need to say the right thing.

"I'm afraid I've been very indiscreet, Doctor."

"Who hasn't at one time or another, Thelma?"

"Not as I was. I don't even know how to tell you."

He smiled and there was a sincere kindliness in his eyes. "Usually when a woman talks about being terribly indiscreet, it means that she's had an affair of some sort with a man. That it?"

"Partly."

"With the one they've arrested?"

"Yes."

"Your rooms were next to each other. Propinquity has resulted in more than one affair. You don't think this shocks me, do you, Thelma? In this office? The things I've heard from women sitting in that chair? Why don't you just forget it?"

"There's more to it than that, Doctor. He was interested in photography and persuaded me to pose for him."

"In the nude, I assume."

She nodded.

"Then he had an eye for a very good-looking model," he smiled.

"He took another picture when I didn't know about it. Of both of us. He had the camera fixed. I'm so ashamed and—"

"You don't have to tell me about it, Thelma. You didn't in the first place."

"The landlady asked me to move. She saw the pictures. And she's going to call you today and tell you about me. She doesn't think I should be in a doctor's office ... or even associating with decent people. So I had to tell you before she called. If you want me to leave, I'll understand, Doctor."

"Where are the pictures now?"

She told him and explained that Lieutenant Martin was going to try to keep them from being viewed.

"Then you shouldn't have anything to worry about," he told her.

She realized that he intended to ignore Mrs. Lindicott's impending telephone call, if it came. It didn't matter to him, and her job was secure. She watched him get up and come around the desk. He gently put his hands on her elbows and drew her upright so that she faced him.

"Listen, Thelma," he said. "You should get married. I wouldn't like to lose you as a receptionist, but you're pretty well equipped as a woman, with an excellent supply of hormones, glands, and everything else you should have. If you land in bed with a man, it's a natural course of events. You should have a husband, but that doesn't preclude your functioning as a female. A desirable one, I might add."

She wondered if she was desirable to him, and at the moment she was completely conscious of him as a man, rather than as a doctor and her employer. If he knew what was in her mind, he gave no indication of it other than a semblance of a wry smile.

"All right?" he asked.

"All right," she nodded, feeling moisture in her eyes. "I'd better get out there. I think Mrs. Lapman is waiting with her leukorrhea."

He sighed and returned to his desk. "Send her in." He watched Thelma walk to the door. She turned there to smile at him, then left the room trying desperately to achieve the dignified receptionist's smile that Mrs. Lapman would expect.

Maybe she *would* find someone someday and marry him. And maybe she could keep her job with Doctor after she was married. She greeted Mrs. Lapman cheerfully.

"Doctor will see you now, Mrs. Lapman," she smiled.

"My, it's always so nice to see you, Miss Jorgson. You're such a *happy* person!"

CHAPTER TWENTY-TWO
MARY JO CAMMAN

U sually they slept late Sunday mornings and it was almost ten when Mary Jo got up this Sunday morning. Bill still slept soundly. He had returned from his trip south after midnight, tired, and with a headache from a long drive. She had fixed him something to eat and after a hot bath he had gone to bed and immediately to sleep.

She listened to his deep breathing as she got into a robe. One of his arms was outstretched, the hand tightly knotted. He didn't sleep easily, she thought. He never had. She wondered if he was dreaming, and what in a dream would make him clench his fist.

As she knotted her robe she looked at herself in the long mirror. Lately it was as if she were studying a stranger in the mirror, and she looked for outward visible signs of the changes she felt within herself.

She was suddenly conscious of the fullness of her breasts, the curve of hip and thigh, the attributes of womanhood that made her desirable to men.

This appraisal of herself was the result, she knew, of the revelation that men did desire her, and that in the taking of her they found deep pleasure.

Feeling oddly content, she left the bedroom and hurried down the stairs.

She put coffee on the stove and went out for the morning newspaper. She glanced at headlines until the coffee was ready, then filled two cups and took them upstairs on a tray.

Bill was awake and stretching sleepily. He saw the coffee with a smile of pleasure and sat up in bed.

"Good deal!" he said. "I was really bushed last night."

He tasted the coffee with relish and leaned back against a bunched-up pillow. "You look extra wonderful this morning. Changed, somehow. New hairdo? What is it?"

"A good sleep," she smiled.

A good sleep! Three nights ago she had slept a good sleep; a deep, sound, dreamless sleep after her date with Cal Horlick. She thought of Bill that morning and would have welcomed him fervently if he had come home.

Now she watched him drink his coffee and felt an infinite tenderness and love for him that was warm and comforting to her. She could live out her married life with this man. She knew this now. There would be no nagging questions about Cal Horlick or any other man. The circumstances of rape, Cal had called it.

Perhaps there was some of the masochist in her, she thought. Perhaps in all women. Not to be exploited nor desired; but in the experiencing of it a woman could well be betrayed by unexplainable forces that swept her into the vortex of sensation and desire.

But she would not want to live with this. Nor could she condone it and still live within the framework of her sensitivities and—as her mother had labelled them—"the standards of good taste."

Nor was she ashamed now—as she looked at her husband— of what had almost happened with Cal. She felt only wiser and more mature and much more ready to be a wife to Bill.

Bill finished the coffee and got up. He went to the bathroom and she thought about him as he ran water for shaving and as she listened to the shower running.

When he re-entered the bedroom clad in a pair of shorts, she had removed the robe and her nightgown and was lying on his bed. He stopped still and looked at her. Then he came to her and kissed her and his hands caressed her soft, yielding flesh. She shut her eyes and accepted his attentions with pleasure, feeling the warm, liquid sensation of passion flowing like warm, red wine through her veins …

Afterwards they lay side by side.

"Good," he said. "The best."

"It's all right now, Bill?" she asked. "Truly all right?"

"Yes. I don't think it will ever bother me again."

She smiled and remembered the deep sense of belonging, of complete and utter happiness that had taken hold of her feelings. Never had she been closer to Bill. It was as if she had been reborn and she knew that she and Bill *could* go on from here and have a good life together.

In the afterglow of relaxation they talked. She told him about her visit from Thelma Jorgson, and they discussed the coming trial briefly.

"By the way, how well do you know Cal Horlick?" he asked easily.

For a second she felt her heart beat hard and she glanced at him with a sensation of panic. He was gazing idly at the ceiling, smoking a cigarette.

"Didn't he tell you?" she asked. "We went to school together. I guess I've known him most of my life."

"What kind of a man is he?"

"I don't know how one man evaluates another man, Bill. I suppose you'd call him a successful man. He's intelligent and nice."

"Carrie said something about his having a case on you once."

She laughed. "A summer romance—if you could call it that—when I was in high school. It didn't amount to much."

"He'll probably be the next D.A.," Bill said. "He'll be all right."

"I imagine so. Cal's ambitious."

"He should get married. A guy like that. It's a wonder some gal hasn't hooked him. He's got everything that it takes."

"Maybe he doesn't."

"Well, compared with a guy like me ..."

Mary Jo didn't say anything, but her smile was secret and contented and she looked at him and idly rubbed the back of one hand along his jawline.

Bill reached to the bedstand and put out his cigarette, then turned on his side so that he could look at her. "Would you trade me in on a deluxe job like him?" he asked with a grin.

She wrinkled her nose in a small moue. "I guess I'm just sentimental about the old model. I think I'll keep you. I get good mileage out of you ... and wonderful performance!"

This was as she wanted it—better than it ever had been. No more questions to be answered, no more doubts.

Bill swung off the bed and began to dress. She watched him lazily and told him she would be down in a few moments when he left to put toast on for breakfast.

Now that the moment was over and she had relished her own contentment, she remembered with a measure of guilt the very real temptation she had had to give herself to Cal Horlick. For a time her body had been ready to betray her. Her experience with Miles Salin had unleashed a latent sexuality within her which she hadn't been entirely aware of. The impulse to experiment with Cal had fortunately not been strong enough to upset her own personal standards of conduct yet, she could not rid herself of a slight feeling of self-abasement for even contemplating being unfaithful to Bill.

Now, however, she found herself able to think of Miles Salin as a human being and not as an instrument of sex and murder.

She wondered about the dark, sordid motivations that had driven him to commit rape and murder. She wondered if he feared death, and if he faced the forthcoming trial with serenity, defiance or despair.

By no rights of moral convention should she think of him other than what he was in the scheme of society's judgment. The murder she could not condone in any sense of the word, although she could understand the accident which had impelled it—an accident of fright and reflex action. His crime against her ... and even against the other women ... could be forgiven. This—at least for herself—was possible.

Nor could she be certain that a woman could ever find absolute hatred in her heart for a man who had delivered her into a complete transport of ecstasy, even if it were against her wishes and despite herself.

The body does not think, nor reason, nor moralize, she thought. *The body so often acts instinctively and as it is designed to act.*

She shook her head impatiently, disturbed by her musings. She must not think this way. Miles Salin was scheduled to go on trial for his life for crimes he had committed. He had confessed those crimes. Most likely they were the actions of a man with a sick mind, but this was not for her to decide.

It was ironic that a man might die for—among other things— the change he had made in her; a change that had not harmed her body, nor disfigured her. A change that might certainly lead to a more satisfying and emotionally rewarding marriage with another man, and a surcease from unrest that might have plagued her for years to come.

Stop thinking this way, she whispered to herself. *Stop it/*

She got up hurriedly, dressed and ran down the stairs. Bill was buttering toast in the kitchen.

She stopped in the doorway and stared at him. How could she possibly have been so careless? Yet the thought had not occurred to her until this moment. Bill glanced up and saw the expression on her face.

"What's the matter, darling?" he asked. "Remember something you forgot to do?"

"Very much so! Bill ... I could be suddenly pregnant. I forgot, and it's a bad time. Oh, Bill!"

He grinned at her before he bit into a piece of toast.

"So?" he said. He went to her and took her by a hand and led her to the kitchen table and sat her down. He handed her a piece of toast and gravely said, "It happens in the very best of families."

CHAPTER TWENTY-THREE
MAX SINTO

Saturday night was a bore, as usual. A cold winter rain slashed across the windows of the newsroom and in the wire service's glassed-off office a young and new employee worried about his first night alone on the wire. He was working for Bill Camman this night.

Max wrote a headline for a local story and slugged it. He tossed the story on his desk and got up and walked to the drinking fountain at the end of the office. The water tasted warm. He lit a cigarette and returned to his desk. Maybe he could finish the Salin story for the magazine. They wanted it by the middle of the week and he certainly could use a fast $300.

He checked the electric clock. It still was early enough to call Dr. Kentman. A few medical comments would dress up the story, and he knew the doctor well enough to try for a statement. He dialed the number and Kentman seemed cordial over the wire.

"It's about the Salin case," Sinto told him. "I'm doing a magazine story and I'd like a comment, if you'll give me one."

"I don't know what you want, Max."

"Whether you really thought he was sane when they had the hearing."

"That was decided by the doctors participating in the hearing. I can't comment on their decision."

"No, I suppose not, Doc. I was just thinking about your reputation as a psychiatrist. It would lend weight to the story to get your name in."

"I'm sorry, Max. You'll have to play it from what happened, I guess."

"Sure, Doc. But off the record, what would you say? I'm just interested."

"The murder was the damning factor."

"Yeah. I guess it was."

"And Cal Horlick can be a determined man."

"Right."

"So you'll just have to write the story from what you know."

"Thanks, anyhow, Doc."

"Not at all, Max."

Sinto hung up and got out the story and read it through to the last page. He still had a paragraph or two to write. Maybe he'd go over and get coffee first. He could write it when he came back.

He remembered his interview with Salin. The guy didn't look like a murderer and rapist, but they seldom did. He looked like a kid who should have stayed in the country. He looked like a kid who might have been a worker in the young people's group at a church, or the nice kid who made good in the village bank.

Only he wasn't that much of a kid. And that sometimes was true, too. That look of youthfulness. He had been very polite.

"No, I don't know why I wanted to do those things, Mr. Sinto," he had said.

"Did you worry about the women afterwards?" Sinto probed.

"Should I have worried about them? I didn't really hurt them. Not the women."

"But you were going to kill Miss Jorgson and Mrs. Camman, weren't you?"

"I guess so. How else could I have kept my identity a secret?" He looked thoughtful. "Killing Mrs. Camman—I didn't like that idea."

Sinto caught the thoughtful expression. "Why not, Miles?"

"I liked her."

"You mean sexually?"

"Listen, I think we'd better call this off. You want answers to questions like that, and you're not going to get them."

"Okay. Forget it. I didn't mean it that way."

"No dice, mister. The interview is over."

Salin had refused to talk after that, and Max remembered the single comment about Bill Camman's wife, and tried not to think about it.

But when you knew Mary Jo and how she was stacked, a man couldn't help but wonder how it would be. Well, someone besides Bill Camman knew!

"Jesus! I'm getting a polluted, filthy mind on this night side!" he told himself. "Get out of the gutter, Sinto."

He left his desk and went to the wire service room.

"How's it going, kid?"

The new young man looked up at Sinto and smiled weakly. He was round-faced and looked very young. "Okay, I guess."

"If you need any help, let me know."

"Sure. I guess there isn't really very much for me to do. Just some rewrites for the late radio wire."

"You'll do all right."

The young man nodded and looked at the story in his machine.

"Maybe you could check this lead for me. It's the only important state story I have, and I never had to do one like this before." He pulled the sheet from the typewriter and handed it to Sinto.

Max read it aloud:

"This afternoon at 3:00 P.M., Miles Salin, confessed murderer and rapist, paid for his crimes against society in the gas chamber at the state penitentiary ..."

Max nodded and returned the story to the young man.

"Okay," he said.

He stretched and yawned and looked at the rain driving against a window.

"Saturday night," he said. "Let's go out and get some coffee."

THE END

www.ingramcontent.com/pod-product-compliance
Lightning Source LLC
Chambersburg PA
CBHW030125260626
47156CB00008B/2792